W9-CUA-609

PENPAL

by

Dathan Auerbach

1000Vultures

1000VULTURES FIRST EDITION

Copyright © 2012 by Dathan Auerbach

All rights reserved. Published in the United States by 1000Vultures.

This is a work of fiction. Any resemblance to actual persons, living or dead, events, or locales is entirely coincidental.

ISBN 13: 978-0-9855455-0-5

ISBN 10: 098554550X

www.1000Vultures.com

www.facebook.com/1000Vultures

1000Vultures@gmail.com

Title & chapter heading font by Chris Au (www.chrisau-design.co.uk)

Interior layout design & typography by Jocelyn Michaud
(www.chezjocelyn.com ; jmichaud@uga.edu)

Cover design by D. R. Tuzzeo (d.r.tuzzeo@gmail.com)

ACKNOWLEDGMENTS

Thank you, D. R. Tuzzeo (d.r.tuzzeo@gmail.com), for letting me take advantage of your talent and generosity. The quality of the cover of this book, and virtually every visual component of this entire project, is the result of your hard work. I am indebted to you.

Jamie Stephens, you are a beautiful person. Thank you for listening to my ideas and helping me with every step.

Thank you, Carolyn Nowak, for providing your talents as an illustrator for the promotional cards for this project. You do amazing work. (www.carolyncnowak.com)

Brian Gowin, you saw what I could not see. Thank you for lending me your sharp eye and catching my mistakes.

Thank you, Mercedes Krimme, for your feedback and help.

Lee Wasdin, thank you for your contribution to this project and to my life; both are better off for it.

Jocelyn Michaud, thank you for your limitless patience and exceptional skill in working with me to format the interior of this book.

To the "NoSleep" community of reddit.com – you pushed me to where I otherwise might not have gone. Were it not for your endless support, encouragement, questions, and praise, I feel confident in saying that this book would not exist. I thank each of you from the bottom of my heart.

SPECIAL THANKS TO MY KICKSTARTER.COM SUPPORTERS
Were it not for your assistance,
this project would have buried me.

AwesomeJamie
Philip Foord
Cody T. Smith
Panji "Gooner" Wisesa
Conrad Pankoff
Meghan Spector
Barbara Boyd
Garrett B. Donleycott
Adam "Gaunten" Nilsson
Mark Thomas McLaughlin
Thomas Polakovics
Colin Arnoldus
Scott Christopher Morris
Mat Jenkins
Janet Amemiya
Adam Rains
Courtney Lee Mollison
Brian Ellis

This book is dedicated to my mother

Penpal

MEMORIES

When I was younger, I took a job at a deli that had what the owner called an "ice cream buffet." On Thursdays, children would get a free ice cream cone with their meals, and they could pick any one of the fifteen flavors we had. There were many times when a child had some understandable degree of difficulty selecting their preferred scoop, but eventually each kid would happily make their choice when the mom or dad urged them along – except, that is, for one little girl.

She couldn't have been more than six, and when her father picked her up so that she could see through the glass, her face lit up as her eyes moved over all the different kinds of ice cream that were on display. When her dad asked her which flavor she wanted, she must have ignored the fact that he was not speaking about a plurality of scoops, and she excitedly named some and pointed to others. Gradually, the realization began to set in that she could only choose one kind of ice cream, and as I watched her try to pick just one flavor, I could see how anxious she was becoming. It wasn't greed that beset her; it was the result of wanting many things equally but not having the emotional resources to settle arbitrarily on just one.

As the anxiety consumed her, she began to cry. There was no tantrum. She didn't yell or pout. She simply could not choose. As her father was comforting her, I caught his eye and made a gesture. He nodded, and after a few seconds I leaned over the counter and called to her as I extended my hand. The little girl looked up to see me holding a cone towering with five different scoops of ice cream. Her mood was transformed instantly, and I can say with all sincerity that I have never seen another human being in such a state of pure jubilation. The father thanked me and saw to it that the girl did as well. They left, and we all moved on with our lives.

That was years ago, though my mind returns to that day for different reasons now and again. Most of the time I just think about how happy she was; but sometimes I think about how, despite her seemingly limitless joy that day, in all likelihood she probably doesn't remember me or the ice cream. This doesn't bother me. As children we have terrific and terrible times – events that, as we experience them, seem to be the most important things that have ever happened to us – but more often than not we forget them. Truth to tell, at any point in our lives we've forgotten more than we know about our own history. The world moves on, and so do we, and what was once important fades away.

But that's just the nature of memory. The events of our lives unfold linearly, but in the mental reel of these past experiences, most of the frames that haven't been completely stolen by time are left distorted and blurred by it. When you try to reconstruct the series, you find that it isn't complete, but maybe this never really bothers you, because you can't miss what you don't remember.

We all have voids in our narratives – lost time that we attempt to reclaim with best guesses. Most people have whole parts of their stories that they don't realize are patchworks of guesswork, and those who do realize it aren't likely to care. We want so badly to be happy – to live the kinds of lives that we always hoped we'd live – that we give gifts to ourselves by remembering things not as they were, but as we wish they were.

Our loved ones pass away or simply leave our lives forever too soon, and we think to ourselves, "I wasn't ready for you to leave. It just wasn't time," because we're never truly ready, because it's never truly time. So we keep them in our memories. And when we regret that we don't have more memories of them, maybe our minds give us more gifts; gradually we find ourselves remembering them being with us in times and places that they couldn't have been, and gradually we stop correcting ourselves because, well, we *want* them to have been there.

Some memories slip away through the cracks of our minds, but leave fibers behind so that we know there's something missing. But this isn't all bad. In fact, if we remembered every detail of every day, we might find ourselves so fixated on the past that most of our memories would be of us just sitting in a dark room thinking about all of our yesterdays – too focused on what was to care at all about what will be. And what of bad things? What of those things that we would wish had never happened if we could remember them? Sometimes forgetting is the gift that we give ourselves, and when we do, it's back to the void, and it's time for more guesses toward a better life.

But sometimes you realize that the memories were always there – you just needed to be reminded. When this happens, it offers a previously lacked context for memories that, while never missing, were never understood. This is a special kind of gift. Our lives are so short that it seems a crime to squander any of it by forgetting. Memories extend our lives backward through time, making them feel longer. And that's what we want. So we try to remember. But sometimes, when we do, we wish that we could just forget again.

But I remember.

The story that I'm about to tell you is the product of my own mental archaeology. Of course, like all great digs, how the artifacts fit together in a timeline is about as immediately clear as which things are important and which are not. Some parts of this story I have always remembered. Others were buried deeply, and some I simply never knew about and have only recently discovered. As is often the case, remembering one thing helps you remember another, and as you learn new things about your old life, memories that you thought were insignificant (or at the very least irrelevant) parts of your overall story are suddenly its foundation.

I began reconstructing and transcribing parts of this story on my own, and when I eventually and inevitably had questions, I turned to the only other person who could claim any amount of expertise concerning my history: my mother. Over the course of several weeks, my mother and I had a series of increasingly strained conversations, and it was through these talks that the importance of some forgotten, ignored, or never-known childhood events became clear. Looking back, these events all seem to fit so squarely that I can hardly believe they required reassembly at all. But what we notice in our lives, particularly as children, is so extraordinarily selective and contextualized that something ostensibly benign or self-contained can be transformed, by a single detail, into something terrible and pervasive. You just have to know what you're looking for, and when you do, suddenly it's all you can see.

Here, I've tried to preserve both my thoughts and experiences of my early life, as well as the gradual influx of new information, so that you might learn of these events as I experienced them. Parts of this story were written before I knew what I now know, all of which you will know by the end of this story, but I've kept the chapters as they were originally written. To the best of my ability, I have avoided contaminating my old memories with new revelations, and I've tried to be as faithful to the past as was possible when extrapolating from my earliest memories. What I offer you here is a combination of what I remember, what I've learned about my past from my mother, and what seems most likely; though my guesswork was restricted to gaps that are ultimately unimportant. If I was successful in all of this, then you will understand now as I understood then, and the pieces of my history will fall into place for you in very much the same way that they have only recently done for me.

Now begin in the middle, and later learn the beginning; the end will take care of itself.

– Harlan Ellison

FOOTSTEPS

In a quiet room, if you press your ear against a pillow, you can hear your heartbeat. As a six-year-old boy, the muffled, rhythmic beats sounded like soft footsteps on a carpeted floor, and so as a kid, almost every night – just as I was about to drift off to sleep – I would hear these footsteps, and I would be ripped back to consciousness, terrified.

For my entire childhood, I lived with my mother in a fairly nice, and extremely rural, neighborhood that was in a transitional phase; people of lower economic means were gradually moving in. My mother and I were two of these people.

Those that spend any amount of time driving on interstate highways will see half-houses traveling alongside them. It's an odd sight if you let yourself think about it; two halves of a house built somewhere miles away from where it becomes a home. Everything about those structures has a feeling of impermanence: the wood that forms them is cut where it isn't used and assembled where it doesn't stay; the most permanent things about those houses are the concrete support columns that they rest on, but even those seem transitory in a way. My mother and I lived in one of these houses, but she took good care of it. As a kid, I always thought our house was quite nice.

As I sit here and think about my old home and all the things in it, an amusing and pleasant conflict builds in my mind; I know now that we were poor, but had you asked me then, I would have had no idea what could have prompted that question. My mother must have had so little money to spend, but I never remember her saying the words that tend to become the mantra of some parents when they try to subdue their children's eager shopping: "we can't afford it."

I don't remember wanting for much; I even had a bunk bed despite being an only child. I'm sure that this is the case for many children in low-income homes, but as a boy, despite the incongruity, I thought my home was as close to a palace as one could hope for. To me, the support columns under the house didn't represent what the house actually was – an imported structure on a makeshift foundation – but what it could be. I remember asking my mother if we could make the columns taller so our house would tower over all the others.

Part of my love for the house stemmed from my general love for the area surrounding it. The neighborhood itself was relatively large in proportion to the town itself. Small towns lack many of the luxuries of larger towns or cities; what few stores there are close down early, traveling events don't stop there because they probably missed your small dot on the map, and there aren't many police or hospitals at your disposal. But, to a kid, these things don't matter because small towns often provide a luxury that can't be found in larger, more convenient or populated places: freedom.

Of course, I had rules to follow – I had a lot of them, in fact. But I didn't notice any of them restricting me because I was allowed to do the one thing a kid in a relatively remote area likes to do – explore. Just a short walk from my back porch was a dense and untamed wilderness that I spent some part of nearly every day surveying. These woods and waterways surrounding the neighborhood were my playground during the day. But at night – as things often do in the mind of child – they would take on a more sinister feeling.

The apparent change in the very nature of the trees and the lake, I think, was mostly my fault. One of my mother's rules was that I could explore the woods on the condition that I would be home before dark. To motivate my speedy return, I would play games in my mind when leaving the woods at dusk; my feet moved more quickly when I imagined that they were carrying me away from ghouls and beasts. When I would dream, the footsteps would belong to these pursuers.

Sometimes I'd pretend that a hideous and ravenous wolf was charging through the woods just behind me; I'd imagine what would happen if I stumbled or fell and it caught up with me, but when I concentrated too hard on keeping my balance, it would always seem to ensure that I lost it. Other times I'd convince myself that there was an enormous clutter of spiders descending from the trees above and blanketing the earth behind, and that I was always inches away from being ensnared in a collective web or simply overwhelmed by their numbers and tackled by the sheer weight of their individually weightless bodies.

The thing I imagined the most, I think, was that if I didn't make it home before the sun went down, my mother would be gone – that everyone would be gone, and that I'd be all alone. I always made it back home the quickest when I played that game.

It didn't take long for these games to become a reflex, and the fear would appear without any effort at all. Some nights I would spill into the house so frantically that it would startle my mother, but this was the winter of the first grade of elementary school, so I tried to compose myself and pretend that I was merely worried about getting home too late.

The things I imagined in the woods just before nightfall created a feeling of general uneasiness in me when the sun retired. My home offered refuge from these terrors, but the architecture of my house came to sabotage my feelings of security. The concrete stilts that raised my house above the earth left a void just below the entirety of the floor of my home. Gradually, my mind came to fill this crawlspace with imaginary monsters and inescapable scenarios, and they would consume my thoughts whenever I was awoken by the footsteps.

I told my mom about the footsteps, and she said that I was just imagining things. This seemed an appropriate accusation given my tactics for making curfew, but I persisted enough that she blasted my ears with water from a turkey baster once just to placate me, since I insisted that it would help. Of course, it didn't. The footsteps continued that night, but I tried my best to ignore them, just like always.

Despite the general eeriness that the games and footsteps would cast over the nighttime neighborhood, my life was a quiet one. I had adventures by myself, or, more often, with my best friend Josh, but I suppose every kid has their adventures. The only odd or noteworthy events that I can remember happening were the occasions when I would wake up on the bottom bunk despite having gone to sleep on the top. This would only happen every now and again, but it wasn't really that strange since I'd sometimes get up to use the bathroom or get something to drink and could remember just going back to sleep on the bottom bunk. This would happen frequently enough to remember but infrequently enough to dismiss. In itself, waking up on the bottom bunk never really bothered me.

But one night, toward the end of winter in first grade, I didn't wake up on the bottom bunk.

I had heard the footsteps, but was too far gone to be woken up by them. When I awoke, it wasn't from the sound of footsteps, but the feeling of biting cold and violent shivering. As I opened my eyes, the clashing of what I expected to see – what I had nearly always seen when I woke up in a place other than the top bunk – and what I actually saw, frustrated my senses as my mind tried to reconcile my expectations with actuality.

I saw, or rather my mind showed me, the red, cylindrical bars that supported the mattress of the top bunk, but beyond those, I saw stars. Gradually, the bars melted away and faded from my vision, and I was left with only those floating points of light and the jagged, crossing limbs of the tall trees that arched across them high up in the sky.

I was in the woods.

I shouldn't be here, I thought. The coupling of the woods with darkness was something I had trained myself to avoid.

I sat up immediately and tried to make sense of where I was. I thought I was dreaming, but that didn't seem right, though neither did me being in the woods. My eyes were slowly adjusting to the limited light, and gradually the trunks of trees and the shapes of overgrown bushes began to take form. I scanned over the foliage without really focusing on any of it as I searched for something I might recognize – something that might give me some indication of where I was.

An unnatural shape caught my eyes, and I looked at it for what felt like a very long time until I could finally discern what it was. About ten feet in front of me, resting among a mass of tangled sticks and loose leaves, there was a deflated pool float that was shaped like a shark. Even after I understood what it was, I continued looking at it, trying to figure out *why* it was there. This only added to the surreal feeling, to the point that I was sure that I must be experiencing a dream rather than the world itself. After a while, though, it seemed like I just wasn't going to wake up, because I wasn't asleep.

I stood up to orient myself, and I caught a flash of some trampled shrubs that looked like a path, but the woods were thick behind it, so I turned to look elsewhere. I didn't recognize this place. I played in the woods by my house all the time, and so I knew them really well, but I had only been in them when it was dark once before. I had run through my woods straight to my house at the last edge of dusk countless times without even having to think about how to get there. But there's a big difference between dusk and dark, and as I stood there taking in all that there was to see in the dim light, it started creep into my mind much more forcefully that these might not be my woods after all.

A shiver that I think was only partially due to the chilled air ran through me as I wondered how someone was supposed to find his way to a place when he didn't know where he was starting. I took a deep breath and a single step and felt a shooting pain in my foot. I lifted my leg quickly and reeled off balance, falling back to where I had woken up only moments ago.

I moved my eyes from the terrain to my throbbing foot and saw what had felled me. I had stepped on a thorn. It stuck about an inch out of the middle of my foot, but it only bled when I quickly tore it out of my skin. I wound my arm back to throw it someplace where it wouldn't pose a danger to me any longer, but as I searched for a safe spot, I realized that there wasn't one.

By the light of the moon, I could see that the thorns were *everywhere*. The whole ground was laced with this natural barbed wire. I had been lucky to only step on a single thorn just then, but as this occurred to me, I became conscious of the rest of my body. I looked at my other foot, but it was fine. As a matter of fact, so was the rest of me. I searched over my legs and feet with my eyes and hands. No cuts. No scrapes. I didn't have another scratch on me. I wasn't even that dirty. I cried for a little bit and then stood back up.

I opened my mouth and filled my six-year-old lungs to capacity, and just as I was about to scream for help, my breath hitched in my throat as a thought lodged itself powerfully in my mind: *what if someone heard me?* I held the air tightly in my chest and stood puzzled by my own question. I needed help; shouldn't I hope that someone would hear me? All at once, I began to think of the fiends and monsters that I had imagined stalking and chasing me through and out of what might be these woods. I found myself wishing I had never played those games. I let the air escape slowly to give myself a last chance to use it in case I changed my mind and wanted to yell. I didn't. I would have to find my own way. I didn't know which way to go, so I just picked a direction and began walking.

I walked for what felt like hours.

I tried to walk in a straight line, but there was no path to follow. I made sure to course-correct when I had to take detours around tree limbs that were too entwined to move through or patches of thorns that were too broad to step over. Every time I would make my way past one of these natural obstacles, I would be confronted with a seemingly identical tapestry of foliage, and the feeling of hopelessness would begin to assert itself a little more. I just wanted to see something familiar, and each time the woods appeared particularly thick, I thought I had found my landmark.

Marking the outer edge of my usual explorations, there was an enormous pile of discarded and decaying Christmas trees that my best friend Josh had found once during a game of hide-and-seek. Although he had been driven out of its concealing shelter fairly quickly by fire ants, we would return to it many times to trample on the stray and spherical colored ornaments that had been left behind.

We had many stories about where the trees had all come from, but I assume now that the genesis of the pile was much more ordinary than what we had hypothesized. Whatever the origins, what was left was a tangled mass of still decorated, however sparsely, holiday trees that looked, from a distance, to be a single colossal Christmas tree. This would be the easiest thing to spot in my woods, and if I found it, I would know where I was. But that was only if these *were* my woods.

As I stepped delicately through the brush, an idea began to form in my mind. If I could climb a tree, I might be able to see my way to the woods' exit. I became less despondent and began searching the canopy for a proper scouting position. None of these trees seemed tall enough, but if I could find one that was, I might be able to see a house. *I might even be able to see my house*, I thought.

I stood still and balanced carefully on my now-aching feet. The trees that loomed over me when I had woken up in these woods had been tall, I recalled. But I struggled to remember just how tall they were.

"What about the branches?" I mumbled to myself. I remembered seeing branches above me, and if they grew low enough, I knew that I would be able to climb up the tree. If I could find my way back to that spot, I could work my way up the tree and possibly see a way out … but that would mean going back.

I shifted on my feet and tried to make the best decision. Turning around, I took a few steps back toward the direction from which I had come, and I froze as a phrase echoed in my head:

How far can you go into the woods?

I hadn't been tortured by this question for well over a year, and I stood there a bit bewildered by the fact that it had suddenly come rushing back into my mind.

On an afternoon, toward the beginning of kindergarten, I had come home from exploring a part of the woods that I had never seen before. I was excited to tell my mother how far I had gone, and she seemed – even if she was only humoring me – to be equally excited to hear it. When I had finished describing my journey, she congratulated me and asked if I thought I had finally seen all the woods there were in our neighborhood. I told her that I didn't think so, but that I wanted to. She smiled as she asked, "So, how far can you go into the woods?"

This sounded like a challenge, and so I answered confidently, but none of my answers seemed satisfactory to her. "*Really* far," "*Super* far," and even "All the way" were all rejected as viable responses; after each attempt to close the issue, she would just return with the same question, becoming more amused by the minute.

At a loss, and wanting to be able to answer her question so that she would stop asking it, I asked the only other authority figure I knew: my teacher. She gave me a quizzical look and asked me what I meant. I didn't even really know what I meant, and so I just repeated the question. She thought for a moment and said, "I don't know, let's see," as she walked me over to the map that was tacked to our classroom wall.

She asked me the name of my street, which I had memorized, and she took a moment to find it before touching my shoulder and holding her finger on a big patch of green. "I think these are your woods," she said. I repeated my question yet again; I told her that my mom had been asking me this question repeatedly. As I told my teacher this, she seemed to realize something and took her finger off the map. She smiled coyly saying, "I don't know. How far *can* you go into the woods?"

As I stood there in the woods with my arms tucked inside my shirt to avoid the frigid air, I thought about this question and remembered how I came across the answer; this stirred a warm fondness in me that almost made me forget about the reason that question had come back into my mind to begin with.

I discovered the answer just a few weeks after I asked my teacher. My grandparents called to chat with my mother and me, and when my mom handed me the phone to talk to my grandfather, "Pop," I thought I could have a little fun and be on the giving end of the antagonizing for once. Before he could even ask me how I'd been, I charged at him.

"Hi, Pop. How far can you go into the woods?"

"What?"

"How far can you go into the woods?" I repeated knowingly, although I knew nothing at all.

"Oh. Well, I suppose about halfway," he said, snickering.

"What? How come you could only go halfway?"

And then, as if he had been waiting for this moment for his entire life, he bellowed:

"Because if I went any farther, I'd be coming out!" He began laughing so hard that it transformed into a coughing fit, and he handed the phone off to my grandmother.

It took me a while to appreciate the nature of the question and its answer. I had never heard a riddle before, but the more I thought about it, the more I liked it. I would ask that question to dozens of people in the months to follow.

Standing there barefoot in the woods, thinking about this riddle, I found that it wasn't amusing anymore. However, now it was more than just a silly question. I had walked a long way; for all I knew I couldn't walk any farther in – the last tree might be just ahead. If I turned back now, I might be walking back into the woods rather than out of them. I pivoted where I stood and resumed the trajectory that I had adopted when I set out.

Everything was eerily quiet as I pressed on. The only noticeable sounds were of crickets, cicadas, and the light grinding of leaves under my sore feet. Occasionally, however, I would step too hard on a healthy stick, and its cracking would drive the noisy creatures to silence. I would stand there paralyzed by the sudden hush, and I would hold my breath and listen for sounds I hoped not to hear. When the insects resumed, so would I. Desperate to keep their noise, I trod carefully on the under-growth, but it was thick, and here and there my foot would press down on a stick just enough to snap it; the bugs would arrest, and so would I.

This relationship persisted until the last interlude that I remember. I broke a stick, the insects hushed themselves, but instead of the expected silence, I heard what sounded like an infant crying in the distance. I could feel the blood draining out of my limbs as I listened to this wailing that didn't sound as far in the distance as I wished it to be. I felt a churning in my stomach and a weakness in my legs. Standing completely still and being careful not to make any noise, I waited. But the sound didn't stop. Suddenly, another sound joined the chorus. A large stick snapped just behind me.

I panicked.

I think now, as an adult, the sound I heard that night was a cat in either heat or rage, but I had no thoughts in my mind as I ran veering in different directions, taking as much care as I could to avoid big thickets of bushes and collapsed trees. I was paying close attention to where I stepped, because my feet were in such bad shape, and I suppose I instinctively wagered that it would be better to move less quickly than not at all. I paid too much attention to where I was stepping and not enough attention to where those steps were leading, because not long after hearing the cry, I saw something that filled me with such despair that I find it difficult to articulate its potency even now.

It was the pool float.

I was right back where I had woken up.

I stood there dazed, staring at the pool float. It looked oddly familiar to me now that the initial mental haze that had plagued me when I first awoke had dissipated. I wondered if that was because it was the only thing in the woods that I actually recognized, but that didn't seem quite right. I shook it off and attended to what really mattered.

I had traveled for what felt like a great distance, but I hadn't really moved at all. This wasn't magic or some supernatural folding of space. I was lost, utterly and completely.

Up until that moment, perhaps in an effort to focus on what I could control, I had thought more about getting out of the woods than how I got in, but being back at the beginning caused my mind to swim. My feet had not hurt at first, but they were agonized now, and I had made not even an inch of progress. I had been hoping that these were my woods from the time that I had awoken in them. I had hoped that I simply didn't recognize them due to the obscuring and distorting darkness. But my optimism had long since disappeared, swallowed like everything else by the engulfing blackness.

Had I run in a huge circle around that spot, or did I just get turned around and start making my way back? I realized that even if I set out again on the path I had tried to follow at the outset, there was no way to be sure I would actually chart the same course; and if I took a completely different course, then I wouldn't have even made progress in terms of scouting the area through my original excursion. And although I had pushed it to the very back of my mind, rhythmically, like a metronome, my mother's riddle marched back to the frontlines – its footsteps faint at first but gradually building in a crescendo that became so loud I could think of nothing else: *into the woods.*

As this echoed through my thoughts, I suddenly pictured the woods as a vast circle of trees. As I turned on the spot on which I stood and looked around me, a fear crept into my mind that I might be standing at the very edge of the circle and that whatever direction I picked would just lead me deeper, farther into the woods.

As I continued scanning the landscape around me, my eyes fixated on one of the trees that I had seen towering above me when I first woke up. I looked at it dully – the way you gaze at something when you aren't actually seeing it, despite how unshakably fixed your eyes have become; like staring at a wall when you're lost in thought. Slowly, both my eyes and mind regained their focus, and I moved my head up.

It *was* tall.

I forced the despair out of myself and made my way to the tree, being careful to avoid the thorns that were blanketing the ground. As I stood on the exposed roots of the tree and looked straight up the height of its trunk, I thought that the tree must surely be tall enough to allow me to see my way out. I reached my hand up and grasped the lowest limb, but as I tightened my grip, my arm began shaking. Trying to steady myself, I moved my other hand up onto the branch, but when I tried to pull myself up, I felt my body protest. I remember thinking that night that it was simply too cold to climb the tree, but I know it wasn't the cold that stopped me. It was fear.

I released the branch and looked back to the spot where my night had started. I could still see the place where I had woken up; it was a relatively clear spot in the middle of an otherwise debris-laced ground – as if I had tried to make a snow angel in the dirt and had given up in the middle of the project. It was a strange sight, but not any stranger than the rest of this place.

Fully conscious of my feet's condition, I walked back to the small clearing and sat down with my legs crossed.

"What if there's no way out?" I questioned, torturously.

I was too defeated to feel anything but apathy, and I turned my attention back to the tall tree and the stars above, looking upon it all with listlessness. Tracing my eyes over the stars, I had an epiphany. I had heard so much about explorers navigating the world by sea – traveling to undiscovered lands and building new civilizations. I had learned that they could do this by following the stars, and my spirits rose in a flash as I realized that I might be able to do the same. At the time, I thought the North Star was just the brightest star, and so I looked for and found the one with the most brilliant shimmer. I followed it.

I was careful to keep the star that I picked in my sights at all times. If I reached a point where the trees above obscured it too much or for too long, I redirected myself on a path that avoided them. I ignored every sound that tempted me to whip my body around to confront it, and despite the pain, I surveyed the ground primarily by the feel of my feet rather than the sight of my eyes, knowing that if this star was lost so too would be my way.

Eventually my surroundings began to look more familiar; a network of fallen trees that I recognized as ones that I had used as balance beams offered my first legitimate sign of hope, though I walked around and not across them this time. Soon after, I came upon the Christmas tree pile – its scattered ornaments glimmering dimly in the weak moonlight. I gave it a wide berth to avoid the glass shards that might still pepper the ground from the times that my feet, when they were less vulnerable, had pressed down upon the glass balls of holiday flair and crushed them. My nerves were beginning to calm, and when I saw a dirt void called "The Ditch," I knew that I had made it out; the feeling of relief that washed over me brought with it a smile that was more sincere and joyful than any I had ever worn on my face before.

Despite the impulse to quicken my pace when I had my bearings restored and no longer had to watch my North Star so vigilantly, my feet were in so much pain that I had to be mindful of each step. A distance I had covered in mere seconds in my nightly exodus from these woods seemed to be never-ending. I walked with a limp in both legs in an attempt to avoid putting too much weight on either foot. But when I saw the edge of the woods' dirt floor cut off by the paved cul-de-sac of my street, I grew so happy to be so close to home that I broke into a light jog, despite how much it hurt. When I actually saw the roof of my house over a lower-set neighboring house, I let out a light sob and ran faster, wincing with each step. I just wanted to be home.

I had already decided that I wouldn't say anything about any of this to my mother because I had no idea what I could possibly say. I would get back inside somehow, clean up, and get in bed; if I were lucky, she would never even have to know about my odyssey. Anything that I might say would sound preposterous, and the thought of this whole experience reaching its end strengthened my resolve to leave it in the past forever once I finally shut that door behind me. However, my heart sank as I rounded the corner and my home came fully into view.

Every light in the house was on.

I knew my mom was awake, and I knew I would have to explain, or at least try to explain, where I had been, and I couldn't figure out where to start. My run became a jog, which became a walk. I ducked under the lowest branch of a large pine tree that stood outside our property, and carefully lifted the metal latch to the gate on the chain link fence that enclosed our backyard. Slowly, I pushed open the gate in an effort to quiet the squeaking hinges. In about fifteen seconds, I would knock on my back door and attempt to explain myself, but I was still reflexively trying to avoid being caught.

I saw my mother's silhouette through the blinds, and although I was worried about how to explain things to her, it suddenly didn't matter to me anymore. I was home – it was over.

I walked up the couple of steps to the porch and put my hand on the doorknob. I turned it thinking that it might be unlocked since my mother was awake; there was no sense in delaying the inevitable. There was no reason to knock. It turned the full motion, and I felt a mixture of both relief and apprehension. I was just about to push the door open when two arms wrapped around me and pulled me back, away from the door.

This couldn't be happening; I had evaded and outran my imaginary pursuers countless times in my nightly scramble from the woods, but this wasn't imaginary. I looked at the silhouette in the window and tried to reach out. The arms constricted around my chest and lifted me off the ground while I struggled against them. I looked down at the appendages that had ensnared me – they were small, but there was something covering them.

It looked like fur.

I squeezed my eyes tightly shut. *This can't be happening!* my mind roared. *The monsters were just pretend!* I opened my eyes again and looked at the arms that were crossed over my torso. It was fabric, not fur, but this brought no real comfort – I was still being restrained. I still needed to get free. I screamed as loudly as I could, "MOM! HELP ME! PLEASE! MOM!" The feeling of being so close to safety only to be physically pulled away from it filled me with a kind of dread that is, even after all these years, indescribable.

The door I had been torn away from opened, and a flash of hope shot through my heart. But it wasn't my mom.

It was a man, and he was enormous. I thrashed violently and kicked at the shins of the person holding me. But even if I succeeded in escaping my captor, I knew that I would also have to get away from the person who had just come out of my house – this hulking figure who was now steadily approaching me. He reached his hand out for me, and it extended out of the shadow that had been cast on him by the porch light just above his head. It was a cruel and cracked claw, badly burned, with the consistency of a plastic bag that had melted and cooled.

Up until that moment, I had never imagined that I could be in any legitimate danger from which my mother could not rescue me. But as I watched the man close the distance between us, and as I felt my captor's grip grow ever-tighter, my fear was joined with rage; my mother simply could not be gone.

"Let me go! Where is she? Where's my mom? What'd you do to her?!" As my throat stung from screaming and I was drawing in another breath, I became aware of a sound that had been present for longer than I had perceived it.

"Honey, *please* calm down. I've got you."

It sounded like my mom.

The arms loosened and set me down, and as the man who had been approaching me leaned down and put his hand on my shoulder, he eclipsed the porch light with his head, allowing me to see more than just his frame. He was a large man, with a tremendous burn scar on his left arm. I broke my eyes away from it and moved them up to his badge; he was a police officer.

I turned to face the voice behind me with hope that was still tempered by fear.

It really was my mom. The dark brown curls of her hair

brushed my face as she knelt down to embrace me. I was finally safe. Tears started flowing down my face, and I sobbed heavily while the three of us went inside.

The backdoor opened to a narrow hallway. On the right was a door that opened to a bathroom, which was connected to my room via another door. There was a faint smell of mildew that emanated from the bathroom; nightmares of villains and ghouls that hid in my bathroom meant that I would never draw the curtain closed when I wasn't in the shower, and would only mostly draw it closed when I was. Because of this, water collected in its folds and filled that whole area of the house with the faint smell of watery rot. To the left were our washing machine and dryer. My cat was sitting on top of the dryer, and I gave him an absent stroke as I walked past and turned left toward the dining room.

We sat at a table that my mother and I used as a dining area when we ate and a workstation when I had school projects. It was a fairly large, square table that had been painted white, but there were several spots where daily use had started to chip the white paint away, revealing layers of different colors on top of the original coat – whatever that might have been. One area looked almost like a cross-section of a Jawbreaker candy – with its concentric and rainbow colored rings, though my idle or nervous hands had helped along that more excavated section whenever I sat at the table to do homework or have a serious talk with my mother. Historically, the more nervous I was, the more frantically I dug. I learned that night that the first coat of paint was yellow.

"I'm so glad you're home, sweetie. I was worried I'd never see you again." She had begun to cry as well. "Where did you go?"

"I ... I don't know ... I don't know what happened." My fear of the whole event being ineffable was coming true.

"What do you mean you don't know what happened? Where have you been? Oh, look at you. You're filthy!" She surveyed me now that we were in better light. "Oh God! Your feet!"

I looked down and winced. The tops of my feet were caked in a thick, dark coat of my own blood that had already begun to crack with the pattern of damaged glass. As I moved my feet against the linoleum, I could feel that the blood was acting as an adhesive, and I could hear the sound of my skin peeling free from the floor as I lifted them.

"You went into the woods? Baby, we've talked about this. I can't believe you."

"Mom, I didn't! I don't know what happened!" I protested.

This was quickly becoming an argument, and neither my mother nor I was feeling up to it.

"It's okay ... It's fine, honey. Just don't ever do this again, okay? I ... I'm not sure me or my shins could take it ..."

A little laughter broke through my sobs, and I smiled a bit. "Well, I'm sorry for kicking you, but why'd you have to grab me like that?"

"I was just afraid that you'd run away again. You had just come home; I wasn't about to let you run off again after what you wrote!"

I was confused. "What do you mean?"

34

"We found the note you left on your pillow," she said, and pointed at the piece of paper that the police officer was sliding across the table.

I picked up the note and started to read it as my mother and the police officer walked into the kitchen. The note said that I was unhappy and that I never wanted to see her or any of my friends again. It was a "running away" letter. While the policeman exchanged a few words with my mom, I stared at the letter. I didn't remember writing any letter. I didn't remember anything about any of this. But there were many times when I would do things at night that I couldn't recall.

I kept reading the letter as I thought about how I would sometimes use the bathroom without remembering getting up, or would wake up and be so tired that I didn't remember the ride to school. But this was different. This was wrong. Even if I sometimes went to the bathroom at night and didn't remember, or even if I could have gone into the woods on my own and gotten lost – even if all these things were true, one thought repeated endlessly in the background of all the other questions and doubts that filled my mind:

This isn't how you spell my name ... I didn't write this letter.

//

BALLOONS

When I was five years old, I went to an elementary school that, from what I've come to understand, was really adamant about learning through activity. The school was part of a new program designed to allow children to rise at their own pace, and to facilitate this, the administration encouraged teachers to come up with inventive and engaging lesson plans. Part of the underlying rationale, I think, was that if the teachers could trick the students into forgetting that they were at school, or that they were doing homework, the students would be more enthusiastic about their work.

Moreover, if the students cultivated an eagerness for school right out of the gate, then the general apathy that has its way of creeping into most students as the years go by could be staved off. To this end, each teacher was given the latitude to create his or her own themes that would run for the duration of the grade, and all the lessons in math, reading, etc., would be designed in the spirit of the theme. These themes were called "Groups." There was a Space group, a Sea group, an Earth group, and the group I was in, Community.

Regardless of the creativity of the curriculum, in kindergarten in the United States, aside from very basic writing skills, you don't learn much except how to tie your shoes and how to share, and as a result of that, most of the grade isn't very memorable. This is particularly true if you enter kindergarten with most of the writing skills that they expect you develop by the time you have exited. As one of the students who was in this position, I find that as I look back now, I remember the people fairly well, but the actual curriculum remains mostly a mystery to me. But perhaps this isn't all that unusual.

I do remember two things very clearly: I was the best at writing my name in the correct way, which I had mastered some time before entering the grade; and the Balloon Project, which was really the hallmark of the Community group, since it was a clever way to show how a community functioned at a very basic level.

The concept of the Balloon Project was fairly straightforward. Each student would release a balloon with a note attached, and then would wait for a response from whoever happened to find the balloon. We would ask them to enclose a picture of their area, if possible, and provide a return address so we could become penpals. The teacher would post each picture on a large map that she had hung on one of the walls in the classroom, and this would help us see not merely how far the balloon had traveled, but how important communication was in bringing a community together.

I remember our project being on a Friday because the culmination of weeks of discussion and preparation for this exciting event made it feel as if I was having a three-day weekend. The rocky start with which I had begun kindergarten had finally smoothed, and I talked excitedly with my friend Josh each day as we eagerly awaited the Friday launch.

The morning of the launch, all the students walked into the classroom and saw that there was a fully inflated helium balloon tied off with ribbon taped to each desk. Our tables were laid out in a grid, and so the balloons had the same arrangement as planted trees in a lot; from the right angle they would all line up, but if you moved just a little to your left or right, they would fan out, and you could see them all again.

We had known about this project since the first week of class, so we had known, at least abstractly, what to expect on Balloon Day. Despite this foreknowledge, however, walking into a classroom full of balloons gave the room the same ambiance as that of a birthday party, and in response, the kids behaved as if it were one.

The balloons were all different colors, and upon seeing this, the students began bartering heatedly with one another for their favorite colors almost immediately. It took the teacher much longer than normal to organize and stifle the students, but gradually we were subdued at our desks and were asked to take out our assignments for that day.

The preceding Friday, the teacher had sent us home with instructions to write a note with our parents' assistance. All of the notes had to follow a loose structure, but we were allowed to be creative within those boundaries. My note read something like this:

> Hi! You found my balloon! My name is ▆▆▆▆▆ and I attend ▆▆▆▆▆▆▆ Elementary school. You can keep the balloon, but I hope you write me back! I like Mighty Max, exploring, building forts, swimming, and friends. What do you like? Write me back soon. Here is a dollar for the mail!

At the bottom of the page, I drew a little stick figure saying "Hi!" in a word bubble next to his head, and after a few moments of consideration, I drew a balloon in his hand. On the dollar that I brought from home, I had written "FOR STAMPS" right across the front, which my mom said was unnecessary, but I thought it was genius, so I did it.

Sitting on each of our desks was a marker, a pen, a piece of paper, and an envelope. The first part of the project for that day was to transcribe the notes we had composed at home, after which we would put it in the envelope and attach it to the balloon. If we wanted to, we could draw a picture on it.

There was a palette of paint with some brushes and cups of water sitting on a long table just in front of the teacher's desk for the kids who elected to paint a picture on their note. It was a sunny day, and those who wished to paint on their note were told to finish by a certain time so the letters could be set out to dry in the sun. Only a handful of kids were brave enough to send their art out into the world.

After the teacher had finished giving us our instructions, most of my peers resumed their rowdy attempt at trading balloons while the teacher began assisting the few students who had "forgotten" to bring their letters to class. As for me, I started on my note immediately because I didn't want it to be sloppy.

My handwriting, at least back then, was quite nice. With the guidance of my mother, I had been practicing writing while simultaneously learning how to read for a fair amount of time before I had begun kindergarten. Since the letter was already written, all that was left for me to do was copy it down verbatim. I had broken my left arm some weeks before, so the plaster cast made it difficult to reposition and steady the paper as I went, but finally I simply laid the heavy arm on the paper, leaned on it, and began transcribing, feeling thankful that I was right-handed.

I took care with each stroke of the pen because I knew that I wouldn't be able to erase. I had never written anything important in pen before; everything of any consequence that I had ever marked on a page was only as permanent as I wanted it to be. But now, each straight or curved line I marred the paper with had a tint of finality in it, and this only served to threaten the stability of my penmanship even more. But this was the way it had to be.

Several years before, when the students were still writing their notes in pencil, there had been a storm the day after the balloons were released. Virtually no letters were mailed back. Although there was no way to determine exactly why that had been, it was suggested that the pencil marks washed out much too easily, and so to be safe, we should use ink from that point on.

I drew the last line on the paper and sat back with satisfaction. I interrupted my teacher's conference with another student to show her the letter, and she approved enthusiastically and sent me back to my seat.

With my remaining time, I took to decorating the balloon. Mine was red, and that suited me just fine; with no interest in trading my balloon for another color, I tried to think of what I could draw on it. I decided that Spider-Man would make the most sense. I got to work and spent about two minutes trying to figure out how to draw Spider-Man's head before I realized that it was impossible.

Deciding that a plain balloon was actually better than one with a drawing on it, I put the marker away and went to talk to my best friend Josh. It usually took him a little longer to write things because he was left-handed and would occasionally smudge what he had just written as his hand moved against the paper from left to right. I went over to him that day, partially to help him, but mostly because I wanted to invite him to my house after school for what would have been our first sleepover.

When the teacher told us to return to our desks, I walked back but froze as my letter came into view. It was wet. I looked around to see if someone might betray himself by laughing, but all of my peers were sitting attentively at their desks now. I craned my neck over their workspaces and saw that quite a few kids had painted pictures. I realized that someone who must have been trying to dry a paintbrush had carelessly sprinkled water droplets onto my note. The ink had already begun to run in outward arcs where the water touched it.

The letter was still legible in parts, but some words were nearly obliterated. Others were simply incomprehensible – rather than being a fan of exploring, according to my letter, I was an avid "explarting" enthusiast. I wanted to know who did this. I felt that I had put more effort into writing that letter than any of my peers, and so for someone to so carelessly deface it was unthinkable. But there were so many kids who had painted pictures on their notes that it would take too long to attempt to figure out who might have vandalized my letter. Attempting to repair, or at least minimize, the damage seemed more pressing.

There was no time to recreate the letter in its entirety. I thought about rewriting just the damaged parts, but if I crossed them out and tried again, my penpal would think that I didn't know how to spell. I reassured myself that there would be other letters and other chances and walked quickly to the table where the paints were. I tore off a paper towel and tried to dry off the note as best as I could without smearing the reanimated ink.

The teacher called us alphabetically to the far side of the classroom. One by one, we stood in front of a wall-sized map of the city and smiled with our balloon tethers held tightly in our fists. The mechanical whirring of the Polaroid camera repeated as each of us had our picture taken. After the film had developed, we put the photographs in our envelopes along with our letters. The teacher handed each of us another letter to enclose, which I imagine explained the nature of the project while also expressing appreciation for their participation in it. The penpals would have been provided with the mailing address of the school and asked to mail their letters promptly so that the project could progress.

That was the whole project – doing these simple things would allow us to build a sense of community without having to leave the school, and do it safely. We would also practice our reading and writing through our correspondences without even realizing we were doing schoolwork. Everyone – faculty and students alike – loved this project, and it had been a huge success every year, with the exception of the year it stormed.

We marched single-file out of the back door of the classroom and into the courtyard outside. Keeping our formation, we pressed our backs against the wall of the building so that we could pose for a group photograph. One of the students, a boy named Chris, had become so excited upon exiting the classroom that, as soon as he saw the sky above, he let his balloon go and started cheering. I think this enthusiasm would have spread quickly if the teacher had been a little slower in scolding him.

"Now you're going to be the only one in the picture without a balloon, Chris," she snapped.

The boy started to cry. He had a sore throat, so his complaints were hoarse and raspy. I remember thinking that he sounded funny, and I suppose there's some justice in the fact that I caught his sore throat a couple days later. I would like to say that in a demonstration of solidarity at least one other student let a balloon go, or even better, that we all let ours go and stood by Chris, balloonless and proud. But this was kindergarten. Most of the kids stood there with restrained amusement, while others advertised just how funny they found Chris' plight. In the end, Chris sulked at the very edge of the group picture and held his left hand out of frame, clutching an imaginary balloon with a frown etched so firmly in his face that it seemed like it might just outlast the lifetime of the picture that he was posing for.

After the photo was taken, we formed a circle around the teacher who said a few things about friendship and community that I imagine went mostly unheard by the students whose attention was now myopically focused on loosening the grip on their balloons' tethers. When her speech was finally over, the countdown began.

FIVE …

FOUR …

THREE …

TWO …

… ONE AND A HALF …

There was a collective groan in protest; she did this frequently. Although we didn't know what this number was, we knew that it was a way of stalling.

ONE!

All at once, each kid yelled whatever their chosen launch word was, and the courtyard became a carnival as two dozen brightly colored floating balls filled the sky. We ran chasing our balloons and tried desperately to distinguish them from other ones of the same color. Crosscurrents and updrafts flung the balloons wildly in different directions, and their human counterparts mirrored their movements on the ground below. Several kids collided with one another as they ran frantically chasing their balloons, but instead of fights, there were laughs.

Despite the ruckus, I heard a rogue "BLAST OFF!" and shot my eyes down from the sky to see Chris releasing a bright green balloon that the teacher had just given him so that he could participate. As the balloons reached ever-upwards, it became almost impossible to track my own balloon, and this brought with it a new kind of excitement. Where would it go? Who would find it? I remember that day so clearly. When I think about it, I can almost feel a phantom sun on my face and can sometimes, just faintly, smell my teacher's perfume. It was one of the happiest days that I had ever had.

Over the next couple of weeks, the letters started to roll in. Most of the notes came, as requested, with pictures of different landmarks, and the teacher would pin each picture on the big wall-map that we had taken our Polaroids in front of. Arranging them directly on the map made it easy to see where the letter had come from and just how far the balloon had traveled. We did this at the very beginning of class each day, which was a really smart idea because we actually looked forward to coming to school to see if our letters had come in.

For the duration of the year, we would have one day a week where we could write back to our penpal, or another students' penpal, in case our letter had not come in yet. Day after day, I arrived at school excited but left dejected at the fact that my letter hadn't arrived yet. There were other students who didn't receive letters either – not every balloon would be found, and this was something the teacher had reminded us of frequently – but this fact didn't offer me any consolation. I worried that all my hard work would have been for nothing, and I started to resign myself to the idea that I would have to write to one of my peers' penpals if I wanted to have anyone to write to at all.

But then one day it came.

My letter was one of the last to arrive. Upon entering the classroom, I looked at my desk and saw that, once again, there was no letter waiting for me, but as I sat down, the teacher approached me and asked me about the letter I had written. She asked me if I remembered what I had sent away with the balloon. I was a bit taken aback, but I told her about what I wrote, and about the dollar, and about the drawing. When I finished, she brought her hand from behind her back and said with a smile, "I think this is for you, then."

I was delirious with excitement, and my confusion regarding her questions about the letter I had sent ended when I saw the envelope. On the back, right over the seal, there was a drawing of a stick figure holding a balloon – just like the one I had drawn. The letter really was for me.

I must have looked ecstatic, because as I was about to open it, she put her hand on mine to stop me and said, "Please don't be upset." I didn't understand what she meant – why would I be upset now that my letter had come? I was mystified that she would even know what was in the envelope, but of course, I know now that she had screened the contents to make sure there was nothing obscene. But sitting at that desk, I was baffled by her concern that I would be disappointed. My balloon hadn't gotten lost. The person who found it hadn't just thrown my letter away. All other possible details seemed negligible and insignificant to me. But when I opened the envelope, I understood her reaction.

There was no letter.

The only thing in the envelope was a Polaroid, but I couldn't make out what the image was. It looked like a patch of desert, but it was too blurry to decipher; it appeared as if the camera had been moved while the picture was being taken. I turned the Polaroid over, but there was nothing on the back. It was just a Polaroid and nothing more. There wasn't even a return address. I realized that I wouldn't be able to write back, and since there was no way to tell where the picture was taken, it couldn't even be placed anywhere on the map. Instead, my teacher tacked it on the side of the map next to the compass rose – out of the way, but still a part of the project. I was crushed.

When I got home, my mom asked me how my day was, and so I told her. I told her I had gotten a letter from my penpal, and she became visibly excited. I think she had always known that I might never get a response, and as time went on and my potential contact remained silent, her consolations shifted from optimism in possibility and potential to realism and acceptance. So, when I actually received something, she was both shocked and overjoyed for me since she knew how badly I had wanted someone to write me back. When I told her that there was no letter, only a Polaroid, she joked that maybe my penpal had bad handwriting and was embarrassed after seeing how good mine was. I didn't think that this was actually the case; my letter had been damaged before it even touched the sky. But my mother's words always seemed to have the ability to make me feel better, so I accepted her rationale, and I felt happy that I had gotten anything at all.

The school year pressed on, and the letters had stopped coming for nearly all of the other students; after all, you can only continue a written correspondence with a kindergartener for so long. This was expected by the teacher, and the lull was worked into the curriculum – our Friday letter-writing sessions slowly morphed into other projects, and everyone, including myself, had lost interest in the letters almost completely. I still thought about the picture from time to time. In some way, I still felt as if I had been cheated, but then again, there were students who had received nothing at all because their balloons had apparently been lost or disregarded. Recognizing this, I realized that I would seem greedy to those kids, and so any time I felt compelled to complain, I would bite my tongue. Gradually, I internalized this pretended acceptance and simply moved on both in appearance and thought – until I got another envelope.

My excitement was rejuvenated fully, and I secretly reveled in the fact that I had just gotten a letter while nearly all of the other penpals had abandoned their involvement. Most of my classmates had written back and forth with their penpals several times, and the ones who received nothing at all were probably the victims of bad weather and bad luck. The first envelope I had received, however, was tantamount to someone laughing in my face; it seemed as if someone had gone through just enough trouble to let me know that he didn't care. Holding the correspondence in my hand validated my objections to the original arrival. It made sense that I received another delivery – there had been nothing but a blurry picture in the first one – this was probably to make up for that.

But again, there was no letter at all … just another picture.

This one was more distinguishable, but not fully comprehensible. The camera was sharply angled toward the sky. The photograph caught the top corner of a building in the bottom left of the frame, but the rest of the image was distorted by a lens-flare from the sun. I turned the Polaroid over, but again there was nothing written on the back. My teacher put her hand on my shoulder and said, "A picture's worth a thousand words, right?" before walking away toward her desk.

"A picture's worth a thousand words …" I had never heard that said before, and I sat there for a while trying to decide if I believed it.

Because the balloons didn't travel very far, and because they were all launched on the same day, the board became a bit cluttered fairly quickly. If a letter came in with a picture of a place that wasn't already overrepresented on the map, it would be displayed, but otherwise the correspondences were distributed to their recipients, so we could take them home as keepsakes of the project. A week or two before the school year ended, the remaining pictures were taken off the map and handed out to their owners. My best friend Josh took home the second highest number of pictures at the end of the year – his penpal was very cooperative and sent him photographs from all around the neighboring city; Josh took home, I think, four Polaroids.

I took home nearly fifty.

The envelopes had all been opened by the teacher, but after a while I had stopped even looking at the pictures. However, the photographs were, if nothing else, a collection, and so I saved them in one of my dresser drawers that housed my other collections. The problem with collections, I had found, was that either there was simply no way to gather all the things in a series because there was no end to it, or there would always be that last item that made your collection incomplete. In my mind, I suppose, the things in the collection weren't as valuable as the completeness of the collection itself.

My drawer was a mausoleum of my incomplete collections of rocks, baseball cards, comic book cards, and little miniature baseball batting helmets that my mother and I would ceremoniously buy from a vending machine at Winn-Dixie after T-Ball games. I put the photos in a box and slid it next to my baseball cards. With the school year over and summer break just beginning, I turned my attention to other things.

For Christmas, midway through my year of kindergarten, my mom had gotten me a small snow cone machine. It didn't make very good snow cones, but the fact that I could make them at home now delighted both Josh and me. He came to covet the machine so much that his parents bought him a slightly nicer one for his birthday, toward the end of the school year. The snow cones produced by Josh's machine were much bigger and were made much faster than when we would use my machine.

Several weeks into the summer break, we decided to take a break from exploring the woods; we would pool our resources and set up a snow cone stand to make money. We thought we would make a fortune selling snow cones at one dollar.

Josh and I lived in different neighborhoods, so we had a conversation about where we would set up shop. As one might have expected, we both wanted to locate the business at our respective houses, so before we even had the cups for the shaved ice, we had our first disagreement.

His neighborhood was a bit nicer than mine, but many of the older houses in my neighborhood had slightly larger yards, and as such, the people who actually cared for them had to be outside for longer amounts of time in order to do so. There were also simply more people in my neighborhood, since there were many houses that stood on fairly small plots of land, and the ongoing construction around where I lived meant that there were always people outside on the weekends.

Josh rebutted by claiming that his neighborhood was

nicer than mine was, and this was a thought that had never occurred to me before. I became indignant, and our capacities to engage in a civil and rational discussion became exhausted. Ultimately, I won by trumping all of Josh's legitimate reasons by exclaiming that it was my idea, and so we would do it at my house.

The first weekend was a disaster. We had both used our machines before, but to be quite honest, we simply weren't very good snow cone producers. We had two bottles of syrup: cherry and cherry, so there wasn't to be much variety in terms of flavors. More to our detriment, we had never completely figured out how best to pour the syrup onto the ice, or how much to pour for that matter, so most of our customers had their hands covered in overflowing red dye when they squeezed the paper cups to take their snow cones away. We made about six dollars and stopped for the day.

We didn't fare much better the second weekend. Josh and I had gotten the hang of the syrup for the most part, but I had the idea that we should use crushed ice in the machines in order to make the snow cones more quickly, since I thought that smaller chunks of ice would shave faster. Instead, the crushed ice became jammed between the blades and the plastic rotor inside the machine and broke my snow cone maker immediately. This machine was one of the nicest things that I owned, and so I became flustered when I couldn't get it to work.

I took the top off and looked inside. I could see the chunks of ice that were jamming the blades, and so I picked up the plastic case and banged it on the table a few times in an attempt to dislodge them. Looking up, I could see a potential customer coming; I needed to clear the jam quickly. Without thinking, I pushed my hand down into the cavity of the snow cone machine and began carefully wrestling the ice out of the space between the blades and the inside wall. I looked up again, and I recognized the person from the weekend before – forgetting that Josh's machine was working fine, I turned my attention back to the problem so that I would be ready for our first return customer.

I could feel the ice begin to give and pivot a little as the heat from my fingers melted it. I almost had the problem resolved when I heard Josh say, "Hey, what's this button do?"

I looked over to Josh and saw that he had his finger on the start button of my machine. Reflexively, I yanked my hand out of my snow cone maker – my middle finger catching the blade on the way out. There was a period of just a few seconds where I thought that I had just scratched myself, but a thin red line soon began to quickly draw itself horizontally along the underside of my finger. I watched as that line widened and spread as blood began dripping from my hand.

I shouted at Josh while he prepared a snow cone on his machine for our anticipated customer, and he said that he was only joking – that he wasn't really going to push the button. He looked genuinely remorseful from what I could tell, though he seemed to have a problem looking at my hand as he apologized. I think now that Josh had a fear of blood.

Josh had already finished pouring the syrup before the customer got to the table, and he held it gingerly so that it wouldn't melt. Holding my finger with the opposite hand, I looked around for something to wrap it in. By the time the customer got to our stand, the blood had welled up in the tight fist that I was making around my finger and had begun dripping down my forearm.

As Josh held the snow cone out to the man, I saw our patron's eyes dart back and forth from the cherry-red ice to my blood-red hand. His expression changed from concern to amusement, and finally he said, "You boys sure have put a lot of yourself into the business!" The man followed this exclamation with a guffaw so long and loud that I could still hear it when I went back into the house to show my mom what I had done to myself. When I got back outside, Josh said that the man had bought the snow cone; we decided to quit while we were ahead, so we packed up and went inside.

It turned out that my machine wasn't irreparably damaged – once the ice melted, the jam was cleared, and it began to work again without difficulty. This was good news, because business picked up the following weekend. Josh and I had taken a substantial break from our explorations in the woods due to a patch of trees that blocked our path, and during that hiatus I made a new sign that said in big, bold letters: "FREE SNOW CONES!!" Josh said matter-of-factly that we weren't just going to give snow cones away, and I laughed as I pointed at what I had written in faint pencil just under the advertisement: "just kidding."

My neighbor, an elderly woman named Mrs. Maggie, was our first customer that day. She pretended to be outraged by our ruse but happily paid us. Before she left, she told us that she would look for us in the lake later that day if we decided to go swimming. We had many more customers that day, and they were all good sports about our trick, including the man who returned for a third time. We made eighteen dollars that day and a little bit less the following weekend.

The fifth weekend would turn out to be our last day of business; my mom would take my snow cone machine away only a couple days later. When I protested, she told me that she didn't want me cutting my hand off, although I had injured myself weeks ago. Even at that age, I thought that this late reaction was bizarre.

Because Josh and I both had a snow cone machine, we each had a separate stack of money that we put together into one pile, and we then split it evenly. When there was an odd number of bills, we would play "Paper, Rock, Scissors" to see who would get to keep the extra bill; we called this decision-making ritual "gaming." That day we had made a total of seventeen dollars, primarily from the same people we had been selling to since we started our business. After we stopped selling for the day, Josh was divvying up the spoils, and as he paid out my fourth dollar, I was consumed by a feeling of profound bewilderment.

The dollar said "FOR STAMPS."

I must have vocalized my surprise because Josh noticed my shock and asked if he had miscounted.

"No ... That dollar ... Josh, that's the dollar I sent!"

"What?"

"That's the dollar, man! The one I sent!"

"What dollar? What are you talking about?"

Seeing the dollar here in my hands befuddled me, and I struggled to compose myself so I could explain more clearly.

"From the balloon! I sent it off with the balloon, remember? I put it in the envelope with my letter!"

Josh pondered this for a moment before deciding what this meant.

"That's so cool!" he shouted.

As I thought about it, I came to agree. The idea that the dollar had made it right back to me after changing so many hands staggered me. I had no way of knowing how far the balloon had traveled, but whatever the distance had been, this was still amazing. Whoever found my balloon must have bought some stamps at the post office, and then slowly and incrementally the dollar had worked its way right back to me.

I rushed inside to tell my mom, but my excitement coupled with her distraction from an in-progress phone call made my story incomprehensible to her, to the point that she responded simply by saying "Oh wow! That's neat!" just to placate me. Frustrated, I ran back outside and told Josh I had something to show him.

We thundered up the steps to my front door and ran immediately to my room. I opened the collection-drawer, took out the box of envelopes, and showed Josh some of the pictures. I started with the first picture, and we went through about ten before he lost interest in looking at poorly angled and meaningless Polaroids. I grew irritated with his disinterest; my penpal had sent these pictures and today, after countless transactions, the dollar he used to send the photographs had landed right back in my hand. This was almost too much for me to take in – the sheer improbability of it all. Even the most minor alteration would have changed things entirely; if Josh had paid the first dollar to himself, I probably would never have even noticed my returning, defaced currency. Josh, however, had become completely disengaged and asked if I wanted to go play in The Ditch before his mom came to pick him up. I responded with a distracted and almost dismissive agreement as I shuffled through the envelopes.

I'm not sure how the routine was born, but The Ditch had become a battleground to Josh and me. Nearly every time we stepped into The Ditch, one of us would lob a clod of dirt at the other, and this would catalyze a full-scale assault in both directions. It probably started with a single, playful toss of a dried mass of compacted dirt, but it became nearly impossible for us to step into that arena without almost instantly entering into a standoff. We enjoyed these battles so much and sought them out with such frequency that "that ditch" became "The Ditch" without us ever noticing. That day was no exception to the rule of combat, but the war game was persistently interrupted by rustling in the woods around us.

We were used to these sounds; there were raccoons and stray cats that lived in the woods by my house, but there seemed to be a little too much noise coming from the forest floor for it to be caused by either of those things. As we continued our battle, we traded guesses at what the source of the ruckus was in an attempt to scare one another – playing games like these gradually evolved into the games I would play by myself when exiting the woods as the sun rolled away.

My last guess was that it was a mummy, but in the end Josh kept insisting that it was a robot because of the sounds that we heard. As we were leaving, I said that if it was a robot, it would have made much more noise, but Josh shook this off and became a little serious. He looked me right in the eyes and said, "You heard it, didn't you? It sounded like a robot. You heard it too, right?" I had heard it, and since it sounded mechanical, I agreed that it was probably a robot.

It's only now, looking back, that I understand what we heard.

When we got back to my house, Josh's mom was waiting for him at the dining room table with my mom. Josh told his mom about the robot, our moms laughed, and Josh went home. My mom and I ate dinner, and then I went to bed.

I tried to sleep, but I was feeling restless. Josh might not have been interested in the photos, but after seeing that dollar, I could think of virtually nothing else. Before too long, I climbed down from the top bunk and took the box of envelopes out of my dresser drawer. I took out the first envelope, set it on the floor, and placed the blurry desert Polaroid that had been inside of it on top. I laid the second envelope right next to it and put the oddly angled Polaroid of a building's top corner over it. I did this with each picture until they formed a grid that was about 5 x 10; I was taught to always be careful with the things that I was collecting, even if I wasn't sure whether they were valuable or not.

I realized that I hadn't actually looked at the majority of these pictures before. I may have paid them a passing glance when I opened the envelope to look for a letter, but upon being reliably disappointed, I would simply close the envelope and put it with the others. As I looked at them now, I noticed that the pictures gradually became more distinct. I scanned my eyes over the Polaroids.

There was a tree with a bird on it, a speed limit sign, a power line, a group of people walking into some building … Right as my eyes were about to move onto the next photo in the sequence, they froze and focused on something that vexed me so powerfully that I can now, as I write this, distinctly remember feeling dizzy and capable of only a single, repeating thought.

Why am I in this picture?

In the photograph of the group of people entering the building, I saw myself holding hands with my mother in the very back of the crowd of people. We were at the very edge of the photo, but it was us. As my eyes swam over the sea of Polaroids, I became increasingly anxious. It was a really odd feeling. It wasn't fear; it was the feeling you get when you are in trouble. I'm not sure why I was flooded with that feeling, but there I sat, floundering in the distinct sense that I had done something wrong. This feeling only intensified as I finally managed to break my gaze and look at the rest of the pictures.

I was in *every* photo.

None of them were close shots. None of them were only of me. But I was in every single one of them – off to the side, in the back of a group, at the bottom of the frame. Some of the pictures had only the tiniest part of my face captured at the very edge of the photo, but nevertheless, I was there. I was always there.

For a moment, I tried to imagine this whole thing as one tremendous coincidence, but I knew that it wasn't, and I sat there stunned. I didn't know what to do. Your mind works in funny ways as a kid; there was a large part of me that was afraid of getting in trouble simply for still being awake. I wanted to wake up my mother. I wanted to tell her that there was something wrong here. I wanted to run into her bedroom and throw the pictures onto her comforter and just shout "Look!" and have her hug me and tell me that everything was going to be fine – that I had nothing to be afraid of. But I just sat there with the looming feeling of having made some irreparable transgression. I decided that I would wait until the morning.

The next day, my mom was off work and spent most of the morning cleaning up around the house. I stared blankly at the cartoons on the television and waited until I thought it was a good time to show her the Polaroids. When she went out to get the mail, I grabbed a couple of the pictures and put them on the table in front of me; I sat waiting for her to come back in. I couldn't even think of how to begin, and I dug my fingernails into the chipping paint on the table as I tried desperately to think of the perfect way to explain everything. When she returned, she was already opening the mail. I heard her throw some junk mail into the trashcan, and I took a deep breath and forced words out of my mouth.

"Mom, can you come here? I … I have these pictures—"

"Just give me a minute, honey. I need to mark these on the calendar."

After a moment, she came and stood behind me and asked me what I needed. I could hear her shuffling with the mail, but I just looked at the Polaroids and told her about them. I reminded her about the Balloon Project and how I had only gotten a picture in my first correspondence. I told her that after that one they just kept coming, but I never said anything because they were just stupid pictures. I dug my fingernails harder into the table and told her that I had saved them all and had gotten so excited when the dollar came back that I stayed up late looking at all the photos.

As I went on in my explanation and pointed to the pictures, her frequent "uh-huh's" and "okay's" decreased, and she was suddenly completely quiet and making only a little noise with the mail. I had run out of things to say, but I couldn't turn around and face her. I waited for her to say something, but the next noise I heard from her sounded as if she were trying to catch her breath in a room that had no air left in it. At last, she subdued her struggling gasps and simply dropped the remaining mail on the table right next to me and ran to the kitchen to get the cordless phone.

"Mom! I'm sorry, I didn't know about these! Don't be mad at me!"

With the phone pressed to her ear, she was alternating running and walking back and forth while shouting into the mouthpiece. I couldn't understand what she was saying or who she could be calling. Was it my teacher? No, this wasn't her fault. I nervously fiddled with the mail that was sitting next to the Polaroids I had arranged. The top envelope had something sticking out of it that I thoughtlessly and anxiously pulled on until it came out.

It was another Polaroid.

Confused, I thought that somehow one of my Polaroids had slipped into the stack when she threw the mail down, but when I turned it over and looked at it, I realized that I had not seen this one before. It was me, but this one was a much closer shot. I was surrounded by trees and was smiling. But it wasn't just me. Josh was there too. I felt my mouth go dry as I realized that this was us from yesterday.

I started yelling for my mom who was still screaming into the phone. As I called to her more loudly, she shouted more loudly into the phone to compensate, and this exchange repeated until she finally responded with "What?!"

Suddenly, I had her attention, but I didn't know what to do with it. I could only think to ask, "Who are you calling?"

"I'm talking with the police, honey."

"But why? I'm sorry. I didn't mean to do anything ... please mom!"

She answered me with a response that I never understood until I was forced to revisit these events from the earliest years of my life. She grabbed the envelope off the table, and the picture of Josh and I spun and slid, landing next to the other Polaroids in front of me. She held the front of the envelope up to my eyes, but I could only look at her and watch as all the color began draining out of her face, as if something was siphoning the life right out of her. With tears welling up in her eyes, she said that she had to call the police because there was no postmark.

///

BOXES

I spent the summer before kindergarten learning how to climb trees. There was an abundance of trees in my neighborhood, but there was one particular pine tree right outside my house that seemed almost designed for me. It had branches that were so low I could grab them easily without a boost, and for the first couple of days after I learned how to pull myself up, I would just sit on the lowest branch, dangling my feet.

The tree was outside our back fence and was easily visible from the living room of our house. Before too long, and without explicitly discussing that this would be the arrangement, my mother and I developed a routine where I would go play on the tree when she would watch her TV shows, since she could easily see me while she did other things. This was unlike our trips to the YMCA pool where I would insist that she watch every moment of my amazing ability to keep my head under water – sometimes for up to ten minutes; she never seemed that impressed, though I think it was because I was breathing the entire time through a snorkel.

As the summer passed, my abilities grew. Dangling my feet while sitting on a branch quickly lost its appeal, so I had begun to move up the branches, and before too long, I was climbing fairly high. As I climbed farther up the tree, I discovered that its branches not only got thinner but also more widely spaced, and so eventually I reached a point where I couldn't actually climb any higher. This meant that the game had to change; I began to concentrate on speed, and in the end, I could reach my highest branch in twenty-five seconds.

In my mind, I was quite a skilled climber, but my expertise was specialized. I only ever climbed that particular tree, and I always took the same path – I had worn off the bark on some of the branches from the grinding of my shoes and the wringing of my hands as I moved from one branch to another in the same, familiar path.

I got too confident, and one afternoon I tried to step from a branch before I had firmly grasped the next one. I fell about twenty feet, and when I hit the earth, all the air was violently pushed out of my lungs. Dazed, I attempted to get up, but as I put more weight on my left arm, it failed me, and I fell back to the ground. When I looked at the arm that had betrayed me, I understood that I had simply asked too much of it; my forearm was twisted and bent like my tree's roots, and when I tried to move my fingers, I found that they either all moved together or not at all.

My mom was running toward me yelling something, and I remember her sounding like she was underwater – I don't recall what she said, but I do remember being surprised by just how white my bone was.

I couldn't climb trees any more after that.

I was going to start kindergarten with a cast and wouldn't even have any friends to sign it. My mother and I had put a great deal of preparation into making my first day of school a success, but we weren't prepared for this. She must have felt terrible, because the day before I started school, she brought home a kitten. He was just a baby and was striped with tan and white; and he was a talker – the soundtrack of my excitement was a never-ending series of short but continuous cries.

The cat squirmed a little in my mom's arms and fanned his toes as he extended his legs. She kissed him on the head and bent toward the floor to release him. As soon as she put him down, he crawled into an empty case of soda that was sitting on the floor. I named him Boxes.

Boxes was only an outside cat when he escaped. Some time long before I was born, my mom had a cat that had apparently decimated the furniture. In the interest of having both a cat and places to sit, my mom had Boxes declawed. As a result, we did our best to keep him inside. Despite our best efforts, he would still escape every now and then, and we'd find him somewhere in the backyard chasing some kind of bug or lizard.

Most of the time his prey would simply elude him the old-fashioned way, but there were a couple times when I approached Boxes in the backyard and saw that he had pinned some poor, small animal. But without fail, the tiny creature would pull itself forward and slide through Boxes' clawless paws, and he would watch in horrified disbelief as his prize literally slipped through his fingers.

Boxes could sometimes be as evasive as the lizards he stalked, but we'd always catch him and carry him back inside. He'd scramble to look back over my shoulder, meowing the whole way – I told my mom that it was because he was planning his strategy for next time and warning the lizards that he'd be back. Once we were back inside, we'd give him some tuna fish.

Partly due to this ritual, Boxes learned what the sound of the electric can-opener might signal, and he would come running whenever he heard it. Most of the time my mother wasn't opening cans of tuna, but Boxes would howl until she put the can on the ground for him. He would smell it and then look up at her in disgust, as if he was thinking, "What is this? *Soup*?"

This can-opener conditioning came in handy, because toward the end of our time in that house, Boxes would get out much more often. He would run into the crawlspace under the house where neither my mom nor I wanted to follow because it was cramped and probably festering with bugs and rodents. We attempted to get him out by calling his name, but when that failed, it seemed that we might just have to wait for him to come out on his own accord. Ingeniously, my mom thought to hook the can-opener to an extension cord and run it just outside the opening that Boxes had gone through. Each time, he would inevitably emerge with his loud meows, while causing a miniature sandstorm as he shook the dirt out of his fur. He would look up at us, excited by the sound and then horrified at how we could orchestrate such a cruel ruse – a can-opener with no tuna made no sense to Boxes.

The last time he escaped to under the house was actually our last day in it. The summer between first and second grade had just started, and our house had already been on the market for a couple months. I didn't want to move, and I protested as sincerely as I could, but my mother told me that the schools were better elsewhere. Of course, I didn't care about that, but there was no discussion to be had. My mom had already found a new house in another part of the city, so we had begun packing our things slowly so that we'd be ready to move when our house finally sold.

We didn't have much, and I had already packed up all my clothes at my mom's request – she could tell that I was really sad about moving, and so she wanted the transition to be smooth for me. I guess she thought that having my clothes in the box would gently reinforce the idea that we were moving, and if it all happened gradually enough, it might be easier for me to accept it once the day finally came. I guess it worked in a way; but even after months of having my clothes all packed up, the room still felt like my room.

A little over a week before we were supposed to move, we were carrying some of our things out to the car when Boxes seized the opportunity and ran full-tilt into the yard. My mom scrambled to catch him, but the cat evaded her and ran under the house. She cursed that she had already packed the can-opener and wasn't sure where it was, and she tried hope-lessly to lure him out by calling him while I pretended to go look for the can-opener so that I wouldn't have to go under the house in pursuit. Eventually my mom, probably completely aware of my little scam, moved one of the panels on the side of the house and went into the crawlspace.

I stood outside the opening, listening to my mother's rust-ling under the house. "Watch for him!" she called to me, and so I crouched down just in front of the hole, ready to catch Boxes if he ran out. "C'mere!" my mother roared, and I heard Boxes howl as he often would when he was caught.

My mom came out with Boxes quickly and seemed unnerved, which made me feel even better about not having had to go in myself. She took him inside and made some phone calls while I sat on the bottom bunk of my bed and played with a Ninja Turtle action figure. I waited eagerly for Josh's parents to drop him off so we could play.

A couple minutes later, my mother came into my room. She was still covered in dirt from having crawled under the house, and when she moved, I could sometimes see the dirt break loose from her skin and rain down onto the carpet of my floor. The unhinged look in her eyes was still there, and, holding the phone tightly in her hand, she told me that she had spoken to the realtor and we were going to move into the other house right away. She said it as if it was excellent news, but I had thought that we had more time in the house – we weren't supposed to move until the end of the next week, and it was only Tuesday.

We weren't even finished packing yet, but my mom said sometimes it was just easier to replace things than pack them and haul them all over the city. I didn't even get to grab the rest of my boxed clothes as my mom ushered me out of my room and out the back door. "What about Josh?" I protested. "What about him?" she snapped. I reminded her that he was supposed to come over later that day, and she said that we would have to reschedule our play-date. When I asked if I could at least call him to say goodbye, she said that I could just call him from our new house.

We left in the moving van, and I watched my home and my entire life slide out of sight as we rounded the bend and exited the neighborhood.

I had left my home behind, but I managed to stay in touch with Josh over the next several years; which was surprising since we no longer went to the same school. Our parents weren't close friends, but they knew that we were, and so they would accommodate our desire to see one another by driving us back and forth for sleepovers – sometimes every weekend. The distance did little to weaken the strength of our friendship. As a matter of fact, in many ways our bond actually grew stronger; being farther apart meant that nurturing the friendship was no longer as easy as a taking a five minute car ride or waiting a couple extra stops in the school bus. We had to work to stay friends now, and I think that helped us appreciate what we had.

At Christmas, after the summer that I moved away, I got a number of presents, but only one that I really remember. I unwrapped a box and opened it to see a walkie-talkie. It wasn't in any kind of packaging, and the cold, utilitarian design stood in sharp contrast to the brightly-colored tissue paper that lay under it. I gave my mom a quizzical and confused look as I picked it up. It was a little heavy for me, and it seemed pretty sturdy. As I ran my eyes over its knobs and buttons, my mom smiled and told me to give it a try while tapping the rectangular protrusion on the side of the walkie. I depressed the button and spoke.

Hello?

I waited, but there was no response. I looked back up at my mom who knelt down and looked at the top of the walkie-talkie and then at a piece of paper she had in her hand. She turned one of the knobs and told me to try it again.

Hello?

I waited again, but it was still silent. I was starting to think that she might be playing a trick on me when the sound of static suddenly burst through the speaker on the walkie. The acoustic fuzz soon gave way to a voice.

Hey! You there?!

Josh?!

Yeah, man! This is so cool!

I looked up at my mom, and she was looking down at me with a warm smile on her face. Josh was still chattering away on the walkie-talkie – his sentences awkwardly punctuated in the middle by sharp pulses of static. My mom said, "Merry Christmas," and bent down to hug me.

Our parents had pooled their money to get us these walkie-talkies. They were very nice – too nice for boys in the second grade – and were advertised to work across a range that extended past the distance between our houses; they also had batteries that could last for days if the walkie-talkie was on but not used. The walkies would only occasionally work well enough that we could talk across the city, but when we stayed over at each other's houses, we'd use them around the house, talking in mock radio-speak that we had taken from movies, and they worked great for that.

Every now and then when I stayed at Josh's house, we would manage to sneak away and continue our explorations in the woods, but these adventures were never sanctioned – my mom had told Josh's parents that she didn't want me going off into the woods. She said she worried that I might get hurt, and she just wasn't comfortable with taking that chance when she was miles away, despite the fact that Josh's mother was a nurse.

This restriction was usually fine since there were a good number of things to do at Josh's house, and I liked being there. His parents were both nice, but were very rarely at the house at the same time since they kept different schedules. Josh's mom was a nurse at the same hospital that put my arm in a cast when I fell from the tree, and his dad was a construction worker. He was a big man, but he also seemed genuinely kind.

He had caught us playing in the woods once when I was staying the weekend with Josh. When I begged Josh's father not to tell my mom, he talked to me like an adult, even though I was only eight years old. He explained why he had to tell her and why I shouldn't ask him to lie. Of course, I still didn't want him to tell my mother, but the fact that he was willing to actually talk to me about it made it easier to accept.

My mom had screamed furiously at me and threatened to ban me from going to Josh's house ever again. I couldn't fully understand this severe reaction, but I didn't want to lose Josh as a friend, so when I visited him, we played video games and played in his room, and Josh and I continued to be ferried to each other's house almost every weekend. I never really thought about it, but the fact that our friendship didn't atrophy when I moved away was mostly thanks to the efforts that our parents made.

Thanks to them, we were still friends when we were ten years old …

One weekend in fifth grade, I was staying at Josh's and my mom called me to say goodnight; she was still pretty watchful even when she couldn't actually watch me, but I had gotten so used to it that I didn't even notice it, even if Josh did. She sounded upset, so I asked her if I had done something.

She told me that Boxes was missing.

This must have been a Saturday night because I was going home the next day since there was school on Monday. Boxes had been missing since Friday afternoon – I gathered that my mother had not seen him since returning home after dropping me off at Josh's the day before. She must have decided to tell me he was missing because if he didn't come home before I did, then I would be devastated; not only by his absence, but by the fact that she had kept it from me. She told me not to worry. "He'll come back. He always does!"

But Boxes didn't come back.

Three weekends later, I stayed at Josh's again. I had spent every day after school walking around the neighborhood calling for Boxes, and listening, hoping to hear him. I could think of almost nothing but finding my cat and was noticeably downtrodden by his absence; he was my oldest friend. My mom told me that there had been many times when pets had disappeared from home for weeks or even months, only to return on their own; she said they always knew where home was and would always try to get back. I was explaining this to Josh when a thought struck me so hard that I interrupted my own sentence to say it aloud.

"What if Boxes thought of the wrong home?"

Josh was confused. "What? He lives with you. He knows where his home is."

"Yeah, but he grew up somewhere else, Josh. He was raised in my old house. Maybe he still thinks of that place as home … like I do."

"Ohhh I get it. Well that'd be great! We'll tell my dad tomorrow, and he'll take us over there so we can look!"

"No, he won't. My mom said that we couldn't ever go back to that place because the new owners wouldn't wanna be bothered. She said that she told your mom and dad the same thing."

Josh persisted. "Okay. Then we'll just go out exploring tomorrow and make our way to your old house—"

"No! C'mon, Josh! Remember the last time we got caught playing in the woods? Even if your dad doesn't catch us, if we get spotted, your dad will find out and then so will my mom! I wouldn't be allowed to come spend the night anymore … my old house is just a couple neighborhoods away."

We sat there silent in his room for a moment before I said what I think Josh already knew I was going to say.

"We have to go there ourselves … We have to go there tonight …"

It didn't take that much convincing to get Josh on board since he was usually the one to come up with ideas like this, but we had never snuck out of his house before. While we waited until everyone was asleep, we discussed our strategy for getting there, while also debating how we would explain Boxes' sudden appearance to our parents if we should happen to find him.

About an hour after Josh's parents came in to tell us to go to bed, we crept out of Josh's room to go find a flashlight. Josh knew that his dad had several, but he had no idea where he kept them; the garage seemed like the most obvious place. We moved silently through the house and eased the interior door to the garage open. It gave a faint squeak, and we paused before pulling it open and passing through the doorway.

I went to turn the light on, and Josh hissed at me. There was no real way that the light in the garage would have woken anyone in the house up, but when you're attempting to be discreet, it's hard to know where to draw the line. Suddenly, all actions become covert by default – like when two friends begin whispering, and after a while they find that their voices are still hushed, but they can't remember why.

It was appropriate enough to comb through the garage in darkness, though; using light to find itself seemed like cheating anyway. Josh's dad had hundreds of tools, and we both squinted, trying to see through the darkness to determine if one of them might be what we needed; if we had needed a wrench instead of a light, we would have been in business.

"Hey …" Josh broke the silence.

"What?"

"Hey man …"

"What?!" I whispered as loudly as I could.

"I can't see anything in here."

"I know. Me neither."

"Do you have a flashlight I could borrow?"

There was a slight pause before he followed his joke with "Get it?" at which point my hands shot up to my mouth as I attempted to hold back the laughter that was building inside me. I had been in many situations before where I wanted to laugh but couldn't; I was a veteran of those battles, but in almost all occasions I could permit myself a faint chuckle, or I at least would have the forbidding stare of my mother to anchor me. Here, my throat clicked and my body shook as I struggled to subdue myself.

I looked at Josh; he was in even worse shape. Tears were running down his cheeks, and he was actually biting his hand to suppress a rising fit. Josh and I stood with our hands to our mouths allowing only the occasional snort and squeak to escape. The more I saw him trying to hold back his laughter, the more I felt that I no longer could. As I sensed the storm reaching its crescendo, I quickly turned around so I wouldn't be caught in a feedback loop with Josh, and gradually I calmed myself down.

As I regained composure and could focus on something other than being quiet, I saw a flashlight sitting on a workbench. I walked over to pick it up and followed Josh back into the house. When we were walking back to Josh's room, I could still feel the rumblings of laughter in my chest. The situation had passed, and I had stifled myself, but just as you can suppress a sneeze with enough effort, the irritants are still there. Before I could even think to stop myself, I began giggling in the hallway, and Josh shushed me harshly as he ushered me into his room.

"I'm sorry, man!" I managed to force out amongst my laughter.

"Dude, shut up!" Josh snapped. "You'll wake up Veronica!"

I had been focusing so hard on not laughing in the garage that, after the dam had finally breached, I had forgotten for a moment that Josh's room was right across the hall from his older sister's. I was so embarrassed by the thought of her hearing me giggle that the laughter inside me died, and with it went the brief moment of forgetfulness about why we had gone looking for the flashlight to begin with.

"You ready?" I asked Josh.

"Yeah. Is this everything?" he said, as he gestured toward the flashlight while picking up the walkie-talkies.

I felt a little foolish – I hadn't even thought to bring the walkie-talkies, despite the fact that this was the one time where we might actually get to use them.

"Yeah, I think so." I responded coolly. "Let's go."

Escaping Josh's house turned out to be much easier than finding a flashlight in it. The window in his room opened to the back yard, and he had a latched wooden fence that wasn't locked. The fence opened to the side of the house, and we crept along quietly as we passed under his parents' bedroom window. We made a sharp turn away from his house and toward the trashcan-lined street. Once we were in the clear, we slipped off into the night, flashlight and walkie-talkies in hand.

There were two ways to get from Josh's house to my old house. We could walk on the street and make all the turns, or go through the woods, which would take about half the time. It would have taken about two hours to walk there taking the street, but I suggested that we go that way anyway; I told him it was because I didn't want to get lost. Josh scoffed at this idea and insisted that between the two of us we would have no trouble finding our way. I pointed out that it had been years since I'd walked through these woods; he waved his hands at me dismissively and said that he doubted that anyone knew these woods better than us after the lengths that we had gone to in order to explore them, even at night.

"But what about when we were kids? You remember how thick the woods get."

"But we're not kids anymore," he responded.

Before I could rebut, he added that if we were seen walking along the street, someone might recognize him and tell his dad;

he threatened to go home if we didn't just take the shortcut. I accepted his preference because I didn't want to go by myself. Nervously, I turned with Josh toward the line of trees across a vacant lot and walked on.

Josh didn't know about the last time I walked through these woods at night and how hard it had been to find my way out.

The woods seemed much less frightening than I remembered. I was older now, and I found that with a friend and a flashlight the trees seemed less ominous and the sounds less foreboding. We seemed to be making pretty good time, too; though I wasn't entirely sure where we were. But Josh appeared confident enough, and that bolstered my morale.

While not infused with the general eeriness that I had expected, there was still something surreal about the woods. This feeling was, I'm sure, at least partially informed by my memories of this place, but there was something about the way the trees twisted together in the dim light of the moon, as the wind rustled and whistled through them, that made it feel like a wholly different place than it was during the day. The fact that a place this untamed was wedged between stretches of houses and neighborhoods made it seem even more bizarre, but in truth, I knew there was nothing strange about any of this. My thoughts were just wandering as I tried to think about anything other than what it was like to be lost in these woods. I needed to break the silence.

"How much farther do you think it is?" We were on Josh's side of the woods, so I thought he might have a better sense of the distance.

"I dunno. A while, I guess."

"Well what's 'a while' mean?"

"I don't know, man! On the bright side, how far can you walk into the woods, right?"

The question reverberated in my ears.

"What did you say?" I uttered flatly, as my feet dragged to a halt.

Josh turned his head back a little over his shoulder and said with a half-grin, "How far can you walk into the woods?"

My face felt hot. That question. I hadn't thought of that question in years – since the night it replayed over and over again in my head as I walked what could have been the same path we were taking now. And with the question now again ringing in my ears, the same panicked feelings that had prompted me to think of it that night as I wandered endlessly through this place began to return. I couldn't think of why he would say that or where he had even heard it. My mind began whirling in a gyre as it clouded with that familiar feeling of being certain that you are dreaming while also knowing that you're not.

Josh hadn't stopped walking when I had, but I could hear him just up ahead of me, and I could see the meandering of the flashlight's beam through the trees. I began walking again and caught up with my friend.

The bush was getting thicker and the trees more tangled. As we negotiated our way through it all, I was about to press Josh about what he had just said when the strap on my walkie-talkie got caught on a branch. Josh had the flashlight, and as I was struggling to get the walkie free, I heard Josh say,

"Hey man, wanna go for a swim?"

I looked over to where he was shining the flashlight, but I closed my eyes as I did, because I now knew where we were – though I hoped that, somehow, I was wrong. Slowly and fearfully, I opened my eyes and saw that he was shining the light on a pool float. This was where I had woken up in these woods all those years ago.

I felt a lump in my throat and the sting of fresh tears in my eyes as I continued to struggle with the walkie-talkie. I didn't want to be there. It hadn't even occurred to me that we might find this place, and once we did, I just wanted to keep walking and leave it behind for a second time. But as the branch clung determinedly to the strap, I found myself trapped there again.

Frustrated, I yanked on the walkie hard enough to break the branch that held it, and I turned and walked toward Josh who had partially reclined on the pool float in a mock sunbathing pose. I didn't want to tell Josh how I had first found this place, so I knew that I had to temper my desperation to leave it. Slowing my pace, I tried to collect myself, and Josh – either in an attempt to light my way or obscure it – shined the flashlight directly on my face. The whole world went white for a moment, and even after Josh moved the light, its impression remained.

I couldn't see anything, not even the hole.

I felt the dirt around the edge of the chasm give way, and I reeled back in an attempt to regain my balance, but it was not enough. I tumbled into the crater. It was only a few feet deep, but it had a fairly large perimeter. I was puzzled. I remembered this place vividly from that night– the topography of this particular area was etched deeply into my mind – but I didn't remember the hole. I rose to my knees as I tried to wind back my mind's clock.

That's when I heard Josh scream.

I rose to my feet quickly and scrambled out of the hole. I tried to see what was happening, but Josh had the flashlight, and its beam moved wildly through the darkness as he flailed frantically on the float. He was panicked, and as the light shot sporadically across his face, I could see it was contorted with fear and desperation.

"What's wrong, Josh?!" I yelled.

But he didn't respond with anything more than the same cries that had pulled me out of the hole. He was trying to get up, but each time he would rise up even a little, he would fall immediately back onto the float, and the whole process would begin anew. I wanted to help Josh, but I couldn't move myself any closer – my legs wouldn't cooperate. I hated these woods. Josh threw the flashlight to free his hand, and I stared at it, still unable to break my paralysis.

It wasn't until Josh roared coherently that he needed help that I was able to force myself to move. I ran and grabbed the discarded flashlight; I shined it on my friend, not knowing what to expect. The light washed over his body, and I could see that he was writhing violently, the weathered and worn shark-shaped float distending underneath him. At first, I couldn't see anything near him that could be causing his panic. I shifted my gaze from the surroundings and back onto Josh and stepped closer. His plight came into view.

Spiders.

There were dozens of them crawling in criss-crossing patterns along his arms and across his torso. There must have been a clutch of them in the float. The closer I got, the more there seemed to be as my eyes became better able to distinguish their small bodies. Josh's hands repeatedly returned to his face to wipe it clean of any spiders that might make the journey up there. His frightened and rapid movements stood once again in stark contrast to my resumed static state. Josh was not really afraid of spiders, at least not by the thought or sight of them, but I was. I stood there and wished that Josh had been plagued by something else – *anything* else. But I had to do something for him; he would have done something for me.

Setting the flashlight on the ground, I ran to my friend and shut all thoughts of the spiders out of my mind – if I thought about them, I would stop thinking about helping Josh. I grabbed his arms and leveraged back, pulling him up as steadily and strongly as I could. Once on his feet, he yanked off his shirt and began savagely beating it against the ground while I tried to brush the remaining spiders from his arms and neck.

When the urgency had passed, we stood there for a moment surveying one another and ourselves; picking and brushing the odd spider off the other, and occasionally slapping our hands against our own bodies in response to some tickling rogue hair or leaf. From a distance, we must have looked like two monkeys with neurological disorders. When the danger seemed to have passed and the spasms stopped, I bent down, picked up Josh's shirt, and handed it to him. He snatched it out of my hands and shook it violently in case there were any stowaway arachnids, and after he pulled it over his head and slid his arms through, he leaned forward and said with the kind of tone you might hear in someone's voice as they were punctuating a great argument with a final point, "Fuck spiders."

We walked on.

I had my bearings back, and Josh knew that we were in my part of the woods, so he dropped back a little and I took the lead. We were getting closer to my house now, so we became more focused on what had brought us into the woods in the first place.

Boxes was my cat, but Josh had known him for almost as long as I had – so long, in fact, that Josh had his own set of stories about my cat. When we were in first grade, Josh was staying at my house for the night and was sleeping on the bottom bunk. At some point while he slept, Boxes climbed in bed with him and was still there when he woke up the next morning. Josh told me that when he opened his eyes Boxes was laying about a foot away from his face and was staring right at him. Josh said, or at least implied, that for a moment he felt like they were sharing something special – that they were making some kind of a connection. This moment lasted right up until Josh smiled and Boxes smacked him in the face with his clawless paws, quickly and repeatedly, just before he dashed out of the room, leaving Josh dazed. Of course, I didn't witness any of this, but I was somewhat privy to the conclusion since Josh's shouts were what woke me up that morning.

That night, as we walked through the woods, drawing ever

closer to my old house, we took turns telling different parts of that story to one another.

We continued on our path, but as we passed the pile of dead Christmas trees, its weathered ornaments still healthy enough to catch the faintest light and cast it away, what Josh had said earlier in our journey still tugged at my thoughts. I confronted him abruptly.

"Why'd you say what you said back there?"

"What? About Boxes biting me on the nose? I swear he did!"

"No. Not that. You asked how far we could go into the woods. Why'd you ask that?"

"Huh? Oh. I dunno. I thought it'd be funny."

"Yeah, but where'd you hear that question? Why would you ask me that?" I was trying not to let on that it had upset me.

"It's that riddle. You told me that stupid riddle in kindergarten."

"What? I don't remember that."

"C'mon. Are you serious? It was the day we let our balloons go. I guess you finished your work, or – yeah that's right, because it was before your paper got all messed up – you came up to me when I was finishing mine, and we started talking about how we'd explore the woods at your house and stuff. And then you asked me how far I could go into the woods, but I didn't know what you meant, and when I tried to answer you, you just kept asking that stupid question over and over."

"Oh yeah!"

Josh started laughing. "And then you said I'd just have to

figure it out, and you tried to be all mysterious. But then you just blurted the answer out like ten seconds later!"

"Oh yeah ..."

"No wonder you forgot! Who'd want to remember blowing a joke so bad!"

He punched me lightly in the arm, and I shoved him back playfully. We laughed as we walked through The Ditch.

We were back in my old neighborhood, and suddenly the task at hand seemed much more daunting. It was probably about one o'clock in the morning; most of the houses were dark inside, and there were no streetlights in this part of my old neighborhood, so our flashlight cut sharply through the darkness, and we saw only what the beam hit. I started to wonder how we were going to find Boxes in such blackness. I found myself wishing we had another flashlight.

The last time I had rounded the bend that was ahead of us, I had seen my house fully illuminated, and there was a part of me that expected to find it in the same state as Josh and I pressed forward and the roof of my house appeared over the others. All the memories of what transpired that night came flooding back. In the woods, I had been hit with waves of flashes from the past from that winter night when I was six, and they would break and retreat back into the reservoir of my mind. But as I retraced my path on the paved road back to my house, for a moment, Josh seemed to fade away, and every step seemed to hurt as if my feet had once again been cut open by the sharp sticks and thorny bushes of the woods' undergrowth. Although I was wearing shoes this time, I could almost feel the small asphalt pebbles that had wedged themselves into the cuts on the soles of my feet the last time I made this journey.

"There's your house," Josh whispered.

I snapped out of my daze and felt a skipping in my heart as we finally turned the corner, about to face the full view of my house. I remembered how incandescent it had been last time, how light had poured out from every window. But this time all the lights were off; suddenly, my feet didn't hurt anymore.

From a distance, I could see my old climbing tree. It looked smaller than I remembered, but my memories of scaling that tree had transformed it into a redwood in my mind. I could make out the rim of branches that were lowest to the ground – the ones that I used to sit on when I first learned how to climb. That tree was the source of many memories for me, and they were all good ones, even the one where I had fallen.

It had been in that same spot years before I was in any spot at all, oblivious to all that transpired around it or who it had affected, and it would probably remain there after I was gone if it was left alone. As my mind traced the steps of causality backward, I realized that I wouldn't be back here this night if that tree hadn't grown, and I was briefly in awe of how all events were like that.

As we got closer, I could see that the grass in the yard now reached half the height of the chain link fence that encircled it – I couldn't even guess when it had last been mowed. One of the window shutters had partially broken loose and was awkwardly rocking back and forth in the breeze. Overall the house just looked dirty, as if a thin film of grime and grease had coated the whole building, despite whatever rain there had been. It had never even occurred to me that a whole house could get filthy. I was sad to see my old home in such a state of disrepair. Why would my mom care if we bothered the new owners if they cared so little about where they lived? And then I realized:

There were no new owners.

The house was abandoned, though it looked simply forsaken. It dawned on me how much work my mother must have put into the maintenance of the house if this is what it looked like when no one bothered; it was like seeing an old friend who had become terminally ill, and it broke my heart. I couldn't help but wonder why my mom would lie to me about our house having new occupants – maybe she just didn't want me to see it like this.

Despite how sad it made me, I realized that this vacancy was actually a good thing. Since there was no one to take care of the house, there was no one to stop us from looking for my cat. It would be so much easier to look around for Boxes if we didn't have to worry about being spotted by the new family. This meant that we could probably make it out of there faster, which was our top priority. Josh interrupted my thoughts as we walked through the gate and up to the house itself.

"Your old house sucks, dude!" Josh yelled as quietly as he could.

"Shut up, Josh! Even like this it's probably still more fun than your house."

"Hey man—"

"Okay, okay. I think Boxes is probably under the house.

One of us has to go under and look, but the other should stay next to the opening in case he comes running out."

For a moment, I kicked myself for not bringing an electric can-opener from Josh's house, forgetting that there would have been no electricity to power it here.

"Are you *serious*? There's no way I'm going under there. It's your cat, man. You do it."

That should have settled the question of who went in after Boxes, but I wasn't going to forfeit so quickly; any chance I had of not crawling under the house was worth taking.

"Look, I'll game you for it, unless you're too scared ..." I said holding my fist over my upturned palm.

"Fine, but we go on 'shoot,' not on three. It's 'rock, paper, scissors, *shoot*,' not 'one, two, *three*.'"

"I know how to play the game, Josh. You're the one who always messes up. And it's two out of three."

We each balled one hand into a fist and held it over our palms. I began the count, and on each word we thrust our hands downward in a stabbing motion until they collided with our palms.

"Rock, paper, scissors, SHOOT!"

I brought my hand down maintaining the fist and held it there. Josh's hands clapped on his final throw. His paper beat my rock.

We began again.

"Rock, paper, scissors, SHOOT!"

I guessed that Josh would count on me throwing rock again, and I almost did. At the last second, I changed my mind and laid my hands together flatly. I looked at Josh. He was pointing two fingers at me as if to signal the number two. He had guessed what I'd do or had just gotten lucky – either way, his scissors beat my paper.

I lost.

It was obvious that Josh wanted to gloat, but he restrained himself; he wasn't happy that anyone had to go under this house. I wiggled loose the panel that my mom would always move when she had to crawl after Boxes. I had removed it myself only once, but that had been a long time ago – I pushed it in hard and then twisted it a little before pulling it out and resting it against the side of the house. My mom only had to crawl underneath the house a handful of times since the can-opener trick usually worked; but when she had to do it, she hated it, especially that final time. As I looked into the darkness of the crawlspace, I had a greater appreciation for why that was.

Before we moved, my mother said that it was actually better that Boxes ran under here, despite how hard it could be to get him out. It was less dangerous than him jumping over the fence and running around the neighborhood. All that was true, but I was still dreading going into the crawlspace.

I turned back toward Josh and smirked.

"Best five out of seven?"

He laughed and told me to watch my head on the way in.

I grabbed the flashlight and the walkie and began to crawl into the opening. Upon setting my hand on the ground underneath the house, I realized that I was about to ruin my favorite shirt. The ground of the crawlspace was nothing more than

95

damp dirt, which would create a problem for the white shirt I was wearing. My mom had gotten it for me at a souvenir shop when we visited my grandparents the previous year. It had an iguana wearing sunglasses and a Hawaiian shirt, lying in a beach chair and sipping a drink out of a glass with a straw. Beneath the lizard in big, green letters, it said "IGUANA 'NOTHER FLY TAI!" I had no idea what this meant, but after about ten minutes of nagging, my mom paid to have the design ironed onto a shirt my size. My mind started turning; there would be no way for me to come out of this exploration without being filthy, and I would have to explain the state of my clothes to Josh's parents. This complicated things; I turned back toward Josh.

"Hey, I can't be the one who goes under, man. It'll ruin my shirt, and your parents will know we were outside."

Josh stood there with a slightly amused but quizzical look on his face. Finally, he answered, "Wait, you're serious? Dude, look at your shirt."

I looked down and saw that it already advertised my activities with thick skids of soil that streaked up and down and across it. I felt slightly foolish. We had just walked through the woods, I had fallen in a hole, but I still pictured my shirt in mint condition. I played it off as if it was a joke and turned back toward the opening. As I moved the upper half of my body into the crawlspace, my concerns turned to other things as a powerful smell overtook me.

It smelled like death.

I turned on my walkie. *Josh, are you there?*

This is Macho Man, come back.

Josh, cut it out. There's something wrong down here.

What do you mean?

It stinks. It smells like something died.

Oh man, is it Boxes?

I really hope not.

I set down the walkie and oscillated the flashlight as I crawled forward a little, trying to survey as much as possible from my current position. Looking through the hole from the outside, you could see all the way back with the right lighting, but you had to be inside the crawlspace to see around the support blocks that held the house up. I'd say that about forty percent of the area wasn't visible unless you were actually in the crawlspace, but even inside I could only see directly where the flashlight was pointing; this would make scouting around the place much more difficult. I tried to call my cat.

"Boxes ..."

I paused and listened.

"Booooxxxxeessss ..."

There was no sound or movement. I tried clicking my tongue against the roof of my mouth, but there was no response to that either. Pressing my hands hard against the earth, I pulled myself forward until my feet slipped past the opening and into the crawlspace. As I moved farther into the void, the smell intensified to the point that it stung my nostrils. If I covered my nose with my hand, I couldn't properly leverage myself in the cramped space. This meant that in order to move I had to breathe the air directly.

When I tried breathing through my mouth, the stench in the air layered on my tongue and coated the inside of my cheeks to the point that I could actually taste it. For the entire journey from Josh's house to my old home, I had hoped that we'd find Boxes here, but now the fear was growing in me that Boxes *had* come here and something had happened to him. I began hoping for the first time that I wouldn't find Boxes after all.

I twisted my body and tried to look around with the light, but I couldn't see much of anything. The foulness of the rotten air now lined my throat, and I coughed and spat reflexively to remove it. I needed to hurry up so I could leave this place. Reaching my arm forward, I wrapped my fingers around a support block to pull myself forward, and as I did that, I felt something that made my hand recoil.

Fur.

My heart sank, and I prepared myself emotionally for what I was about to see. I crawled slowly so I could prolong what I knew was coming, and I inched my eyes and the flashlight past the block to see what was on the other side.

I staggered back in horror and disgust. "Jesus Christ!" escaped my trembling mouth. It was a hideous and twisted creature, badly decomposed. Its skin had rotted away on its face so the teeth were revealed in an ever-present sneer that made them look enormous. Its eyes had either sunk back into its skull or were simply gone altogether, but I still felt like it was looking right at me. The smell radiating from it was unbearable.

What is it?! Are you okay? Is it Boxes?

I reached for the walkie. *No, no I don't think so.*

Well, what the hell is it then?

I don't know.

I shined the light on it again and looked at it with less fear in my vision. I chuckled, though I felt bad for doing so.

It's a raccoon!

Well keep looking. I'm gonna go into the house to see if he might've made it in there somehow.

What? No. Josh, don't go in there. What … what if Boxes is down here and runs out?

He can't. I put the board back.

I looked and saw that he was telling the truth.

Why'd you do that?!

Don't worry, man; you can move it easy. Doing it this way makes more sense. If Boxes ran out and I missed him, then he'd be gone. If he's down there, then it'll be easier for you to grab him, and then you can just radio me, and I'll come move the board. If he's not down there, then you can move it yourself and meet me in the house.

I thought of the times that my mother had tried to catch Boxes either running out of the house or sprinting around the backyard; Josh had a point. In fact, this plan seemed more thoroughly thought-out than our entire mission. Still, I liked the idea of him being just outside, even if he wasn't doing anything productive – it was just good to have him there. But we'd save time this way, and we needed all the time we could get; both of Josh's parents got up early, and I would still have to try to clean my clothes after crawling around under the house. I didn't want him to abandon his post, but there was always the chance he wouldn't be able to get in anyway.

Hesitantly, I radioed him back.

Okay. But be careful, and don't touch anything.

Don't worry, man; I won't touch your Barbie collection.

I laughed. *You remember your way around inside, right?*

Yeah, I think so. Where do you think I should look?

I thought for a moment. *He used to sit on the washer or dryer sometimes, but if he's not there, then try my room. There's a bunch of my old clothes still in boxes there; check to see if he crawled in one, I guess. And make sure to bring your walkie.*

Roger that, good buddy, Josh replied.

I realized only then that it would be pitch-black in there; the power would have been turned off since no one was paying the bill. With any luck he'd be able to see from the streetlights on the other side of the house that might cast some light inside – otherwise, I wasn't sure how he'd find his way around, or how he'd find Boxes, for that matter.

Before too long, I heard footsteps right over my head and felt old dirt raining down on me.

Josh is that you?

chhkkkk Breaker. Breaker. This is Macho Man coming back for the big Tango Foxtrot. The Eagle has landed. What's your 20, Princess Jasmine? Over.

"Asshole …" I muttered to myself. *Macho Man, you know that you don't have to make the walkie-talkie noise when we're actually on the walkie-talkies, right? And my 20 is in your bathroom lookin' at your stash of magazines, good buddy. Looks like you've got a thing for dudes' butts. What's the report on that? Over.*

I could hear him laughing without the walkie, and I started laughing too. I heard the footsteps fade away a little – he was on his way to my room.

Man, it's dark in here. Hey, are you sure that you had boxes of clothes in here? I don't see any.

Yeah, there should be a couple boxes in front of the closet.

There aren't any boxes; let me check to see if you maybe put them in the closet or something before you left.

I knew that I hadn't done that. I started thinking that maybe my mom had come back and gotten the clothes and just given them away because I had outgrown a lot of them. But I remembered leaving the boxes there – I didn't even have time to close the last one up before we left so abruptly that summer.

While I was waiting for Josh to tell me what he found, I felt a tingling on my foot and thoughts of spiders surged back into my mind. I kicked out my leg quickly, and the sensation subsided. There were no spiders – my leg had fallen asleep due to the position I had been laying in. As the feeling returned to my foot, I became aware of the fact that it was now resting on something other than mounds of dirt. I turned my head back and stared, trying to make sense of what I was seeing.

My foot was resting on a bowl that lay among a scattering of other bowls. I turned my body, crawled a little closer to the collection, and saw that most of the bowls were lying on a brown blanket that was quite difficult to see in this darkness, since it was earth-colored. The blanket smelled moldy, and most of the bowls were empty, but one had something that I recognized still in it.

Cat food.

It was a different kind of food than we gave to Boxes, and initially I couldn't understand why it would be down there of all places. Suddenly, I understood. If Boxes had ever escaped our backyard, there would have been a very good chance that he might have gotten hurt since he didn't have his front claws. My mom must have set up a little place for him under the house to encourage him to come here instead of running around the neighborhood. That made a lot of sense, and it explained why Boxes had scampered under there as frequently as he had toward the end of our time in the house. Knowing about this place, it seemed even more likely that Boxes would have come back to it. *That's so cool, mom*, I thought, as the sound of static came through the walkie.

I found your clothes.

Oh cool. Where were the boxes?

Like I said, there are no boxes. Your clothes are in your closet … They're hanging up.

I felt a chill. This was impossible. I had packed *all* my clothes. Even though we weren't supposed to move that day, I remembered having packed them weeks before and thinking that it was stupid for me to have to get clothes out of a box only to put them back in. I had packed them, but now they were hung back up. Why though?

Josh needed to get out of there.

That can't be right, Josh. They're supposed to be in boxes.

I put them in boxes. Stop messing around, and just come back outside.

No joke man. I'm looking at them. Maybe you just thought that you left them all packed up … Haha! Wow! Talk about an ego!

What? What do you mean?

Your walls, man. Haha. Your walls are covered *in Polaroids of yourself! There are like hundreds of them! What'd you hire someone to—*

Silence.

I checked my walkie to see if I had switched it off somehow. It was on. Looking at the frequency knob to see if it had been moved, I could see that it was on the right channel. I could hear rapid footsteps in the house above me, but I couldn't tell exactly where Josh was going. I waited for Josh to finish his sentence, thinking that his finger had just slipped off the button, but he didn't continue. He seemed to be stomping around the house now. I was just about to radio him when his words whispered through the crackling walkie-talkie.

There's someone in the house …

His voice was hushed and broken – I could hear that he was on the verge of tears. I wanted to respond, but how loud was his walkie turned up? What if the other person heard it? I couldn't take the chance that I'd lead this other person right to him, so I said nothing and just waited, hoped, and listened. What I heard were footsteps – heavy, dragging footsteps. I tried to discern where they were going, but they seemed to be walking around aimlessly. Finally, they stopped.

After only a moment there was a loud thud a few feet above

me, and I could hear the dirt and sand raining down from the underside of the floor onto the ground of the crawlspace.

"Oh God … Josh."

He had been found; I was sure of it. This person had found him and was hurting him. I couldn't move. I wanted to run home. I wanted to save Josh. I wanted to go for help. I wanted so many things, but I just lay there, frozen and racked with guilt over the fact that I was failing my friend. It wasn't at all that I was unable to help him – as if I had tried and failed and felt I had let him down. As if I had tried to scramble out of this pit and rush inside to rescue him only to be thwarted and defeated – it was that I couldn't bring myself to try anything at all. I hadn't moved one inch, and he was my best friend in the world. He was my *only* friend, next to Boxes.

I broke out in tears at the thought of Josh's fate and at the knowledge of my own impotency when he needed me. And I cried even harder from the selfish fears that were stirring up inside of me as I realized that Josh might have told this person where I was hiding and that there was nothing I could possibly do. As I struggled to compose myself, I felt my heart flutter when I heard Josh's voice through the walkie, but this relief was short-lived.

He's got something, man. It's a big bag. He just threw it on the floor. And … oh God, man … the bag … I think it just moved.

Josh hadn't been discovered, but I knew he soon would be by the man with the bag. It was hopeless. As I lay there unable to move, my eyes focused on the corner of the house that was right under my room – right under where Josh would soon be discovered. I moved the flashlight. My breath hitched at what I saw.

Animals. Dozens of them. All of them dead. They lay as a heaping pile of fur, claws, and teeth. Time and weather had fused some of them together into grotesque chimeras, their snarling mouths telling the world of their dissatisfaction at the union. Could Boxes be among these corpses? Was this what the cat food was for? For a moment, I thought to move closer. Perhaps, if he was there, I could see him and know the truth.

A heavy footstep above me broke my shock; I knew I had to get out of there, and I scrambled to the board. I pushed on it, but it wouldn't budge. I couldn't move it, and I couldn't get my fingers around it since the edges were outside; Josh had put it back the wrong way. I was trapped.

"God*damn* you, Josh!" I whispered to myself. I could feel thunderous footsteps above me. The whole house was shaking. I heard Josh scream, and it was matched by another scream that wasn't full of fear.

The storming above continued as I clawed at the board. Their footsteps were tracing patterns on the floor and charting a map of their routes in my mind. They ran from my bedroom, to the living room, to the kitchen, to the front door, and around and around. They ran until I didn't hear any more running.

I pushed on the board as hard as I could, and I felt it move, but I knew it wasn't me who was moving it. I could hear footsteps above me and in front of me and shouting and screaming filling the brief silences between the stomping and shuffling.

The board moved a little more, and what little ambient light there was outside poured through this new opening.

Walkie or flashlight? I had to make a decision of which to use to defend myself. It was still so dark outside that I feared I couldn't make it back to Josh's without the light, but if I broke the walkie-talkie, then Josh and I would be separated completely. The board moved more. I didn't have time to wager any longer. The walkie seemed sturdier so I moved back and clutched it, ready to strike with all of my might. The board was thrown to the side and an arm shot in and grabbed for me.

"Let's go, man! Now!"

It was Josh. Thank God.

I scrambled out of the opening, holding the flashlight and the walkie, and we ran as fast as we could to the fence as the long grass whipped against our legs. I was the first one over the fence with Josh close behind me, but when Josh hit the street-side of the grass, I heard him curse. His walkie's strap had caught on the metal tension wire at the top of the fence and pulled loose from his arm, falling on the bad side of the barricade. Quickly, Josh went to climb back over the fence to retrieve it, and reflexively I grabbed the back of his shirt, yelling, "Forget it, man! We gotta go!"

Behind us, I could hear yelling, though they weren't words, only sounds. Without discussing it, we, perhaps foolishly, ran for the woods in order to get back to Josh's house more quickly, while hopefully being somewhat harder to follow. We tore through thick patches of foliage, which tore back through us, albeit unequally. My arms were stinging with fresh cuts and scrapes from the woodland blockades that attempted to slow us down. The whole way through the woods Josh kept muttering,

"My picture … He took my picture …"

I began to feel physically ill from the guilt that this caused in me. I knew the man *already* had Josh's picture – from when we played as boys in The Ditch. I supposed Josh hadn't thought about that day since it happened; maybe he still thought those mechanical sounds were from a robot. Aside from Josh's mutterings, not a word was shared between us as we hustled through the woods back toward Josh's house.

We made it back into his room before his parents woke up. I didn't know how to use his washing machine, and even if I did, it would have made too much noise. After my attempt to scrub the dirt out of my shirt and pants with water from the sink proved unsuccessful, I borrowed some clothes from Josh and reluctantly snuck back outside to throw the incriminating clothes into the large, green city trashcan that was sitting by the curb.

The fact that there were so many trashcans lining the neighborhood road told me that garbage day was somewhere nearby on the calendar, and when I lifted the lid to Josh's trashcan and saw it filled with garbage bags, I was relieved that the day hadn't already come. I hesitated for a second – taking a last look at the lizard on my shirt – then shoved the clothes underneath one of the bags and crept back around the house and through Josh's bedroom window.

We sat in silence for a while, and it started to become uncomfortable. Finally, to break the quiet in the room, I asked him about the big bag in my old house and if it really moved – he said he couldn't be sure. He kept apologizing about dropping the walkie-talkie at the house, but obviously that wasn't a big deal, all things considered. We didn't go to sleep that night. Instead, we sat peering out the window, waiting for the man with the bag, but he never came. We agreed to never tell anyone about what happened – no good would come from that. After a couple of hours, the sun pushed the darkness out of the sky, and my mom came to get me a couple of hours after that.

She asked me about the clothes I had on, and I told her that Josh had liked the shirt I had been wearing and asked if he could borrow it. She said that was nice of me. As we were pulling out of Josh's driveway, my eyes lingered on the trashcan at the edge of their yard, and I caught myself whispering, "I thought I closed the lid …" I considered that the garbage truck might have just put the trashcan down with the lid open, but it didn't matter. The evidence was gone, and I breathed easy.

Until very recently, my mother didn't know about what Josh and I had done that night. Of course, I spared many of the details when I told her, but I thought that if I told her something she didn't know, maybe she would reciprocate. By the end of the story, my mother's eyes had glossed over. I asked her why she lied about bothering the new owners to stop me from going when there weren't any new owners at all – why had she tried so hard to stop me from going back to our old home? She became irate and hysterical, and told me to get out of her house, but I just sat there, waiting.

When she realized that I wouldn't leave, she sat back down, and she answered my question. She grabbed my hand and squeezed it harder than I thought her capable of and locked her eyes to mine. She whispered through clenched teeth as if she was afraid of being overheard:

"Because I never put any fucking blankets or bowls under the house for Boxes. You think you were the only one to find them there? Don't you tell me that I lied to you about there being someone in that house, *goddamn* you."

I felt dizzy. With those few sentences, I understood so much. I understood why she had looked so uneasy after she brought Boxes out from under the house on our last day there; she found more than spiders or a rat's nest that day. I understood why we left almost two weeks early. I understood why she tried to stop me from going back.

She knew. She knew he made his home under ours, and she kept it from me, and as I walked out of her house, I could only think of what else she might know. I left my mother that night without saying another word. I didn't finish the story for her, but I want to finish it here, for you.

When I got home from Josh's house that day, I threw my stuff on the floor, and it scattered everywhere; I didn't care, I just wanted to sleep. I woke up around nine o'clock that night to the sound of Boxes' meowing. My heart leapt. He had finally come home. I was a little sick about the fact that if I had just waited a day, none of the previous night's events would have happened and I'd have Boxes anyway, but that didn't matter; he was back. I got off my bed and called for him – looking around to catch a glint of light off his eyes. The crying continued, and I followed it. It was coming from under the bed. I laughed a little thinking I had just crawled under a house looking for him and how this was so much better. His meows were being muffled by a jacket, so I flung it aside and smiled, yelling, "Welcome home, Boxes!"

His cries were coming from my walkie-talkie.

Boxes never came home.

////

MAPS

Most old cities and the neighborhoods in them weren't planned in anticipation of a tremendous population growth. Generally speaking, the layout of the roads is originally in response to geographical restrictions and the necessity of connecting points of economic importance. Once the connecting roads are established, new businesses and roads are positioned strategically along the existing skeleton, and eventually the paths carved into the earth are immortalized in asphalt, leaving room only for minor modifications, additions, and alterations, but rarely a dramatic change.

If that is true, then my childhood neighborhood must have been old. If straight lines move "as the crow flies," then my neighborhood must have been built based on the travels of a snake. The first houses would have been placed around the lake, I'm sure, and while older, these houses were the nicest in the neighborhood. Gradually, the inhabitable area increased as new extensions were built off the original path, but these new extensions all ended abruptly at one point or another. All the neighborhood streets converged into a single strip of pavement that connected with the road into town; this was the only legitimate way either in or out of the neighborhood. A tributary, which both fed and drank from the lake, limited many of these extensions as it bifurcated the woods before passing right by The Ditch.

Many of the original homes had enormous yards, but some of those original plots, and all of the later lots, had been divided, leaving properties with smaller and smaller boundaries. An aerial view of my neighborhood would give one the impression that an enormous squid had once died in the woods, only to be found by some adventuring entrepreneur who paved roads over its tentacles, withdrawing his involvement to leave time, greed, and desperation to divide up the land between the roads among prospective home-owners like an embarrassing attempt at the Golden Ratio.

Our house was on a small rectangle of land, but we had a front and back yard. This was a luxury that would be eliminated over time as there were some residents who shared patches of land that were as big as the one upon which my house was placed. Even still, developers were carting in and assembling new modular homes, and families were continuing to park their trailer-homes on smaller and smaller lots; the neighborhood had been undergoing this expansion for a long time.

From my porch, you could see the old houses that

surrounded the lake, and while these were all beautiful, the house of Mrs. Maggie was my favorite. It was an off-white, colonial-style house, though it was more modest than what that style typically offers. There was only one story, though a trinity of false windows extending off the lowest part of the roof convinced me that there were at least two. Her porch wrapped around her house all the way to the back where it grew an appendage that moved down a slightly sloping hill and became a dock once it settled on the water.

Like many of the yards with nicer homes on them, Mrs. Maggie's had a sprinkler system that was on a timer; though at some point over the years, her timer must have broken because the sprinklers would come on at various points during the day, and often even at night, all year. While it never got cold enough to snow where I lived, several times each winter I would go outside in the morning to see Mrs. Maggie's yard transformed into a surreal arctic paradise by the frozen water from her sprinklers.

Every other yard stood sterilized and arid by the biting frost of the winter's cold, but right there in the middle of the bleak reminder of the savagery of the season was an oasis of beautiful ice, hanging like stalactites from every branch of every tree and every leaf of every bush. As the sun rose, its light spread through her trees, and each piece of ice splintered the rays into a rainbow that could only be viewed briefly before it blinded you. Even as a child, I was struck by how beautiful it was, and often Josh and I would go over there to walk on the iced grass and have sword fights with the icicles.

Mrs. Maggie was, as best as I can remember, around eighty years old, and was one of the friendliest and sweetest people I had ever met, despite her quirks. She had a head of loose-set white curls and always wore light dresses with floral patterns over her frail, but not sickly, body. When it was warm and Josh and I would go swimming in the lake, she would sit out on her back porch and just talk with us. She never brought a book or a magazine, never had a crossword puzzle or a word-search; I think she came out on those days just to visit.

Sometimes we would swim out nearly to the center of the oval lake, and she would call us back, yelling not to swim too far, but we never listened. When we played close to the shore, she would ask us about school, and any time we told her what we were learning or what assignments we had, she would say that we should be thankful because she always had to work harder when she was our age. I once told her that we were building a spaceship; Mrs. Maggie said that we were getting off easy.

While the last weeks of kindergarten played out, Josh and I found ourselves in the lake nearly every weekend, and so nearly every weekend Mrs. Maggie found herself out on her porch. The Community group was wrapping up the Balloon Project, and on the day that we took our last pictures home, Josh had come to play at my house after school. Though the initial enthusiasm for the project had long since abated, taking all the Polaroids off the map and bringing them home had stirred the embers of our dwindling excitement.

When we were swimming in the lake that day, Josh asked how far I thought a letter might go if we put it in a bottle and

116

threw it into the ocean. We guessed at this until Mrs. Maggie, who was eavesdropping, interjected and said that it would depend on which ocean it was and what the currents were like. She said, as she gestured toward the tributary, that we could even throw it into the lake and it might travel hundreds of miles.

I asked her if she thought the bottle would go farther than a balloon, and she looked at me quizzically as if she expected me to elaborate. I thought she already knew about the Balloon Project; I thought I had explained it to her before, but I told her about it anyway. She said that she had never heard of an experiment exactly like that, and that it sounded wonderful. Her husband, Tom, was a pilot, and she joked that if one of our balloons had been caught on the wing of his plane, it could have ended up on the other side of the world.

Mrs. Maggie said that Tom should be home any day and that she would ask him if he saw any balloons in the sky while he was flying. She was smiling so cheerfully that I didn't want to upset her by pointing out that she had already told us that joke months ago.

When Josh and I started paddling toward the shore, Mrs. Maggie invited us in for snacks. This was fairly routine; she would laugh and say that she had made too much food or lemonade and would gesture enthusiastically for us to walk up the dock and onto her porch. It was a tempting offer, especially when it was hot outside or we had tread water for too long, but we would always decline as politely as young boys knew how; Mrs. Maggie wasn't a stranger, but despite how kind she was, we were never comfortable enough with her to accept her invitation. I don't know what Josh's reservations were, exactly, but mine began the day I met Mrs. Maggie.

The first time I met her was the first time my mother let me walk home from the bus stop by myself. For the first few weeks of kindergarten, my mom had made arrangements with her employer to pick me up from school, but this meant that to make up for the lost time, she would have to leave me at our house alone for about an hour each day. We didn't live very far from my elementary school, but the lines to pick up the students were always long; so long, in fact, that the students who rode the bus would often make it back to their houses before we made it back to ours.

Eventually my mom relaxed enough to let me ride the bus, and she would meet me with her car where the bus dropped me off. Many of the other kids that shared my bus stop, however, had their own keys to their houses, and I would get into my mom's car and watch them run and skip home with their keys dangling around their necks or swinging from their hands. This made me jealous.

I pleaded with my mom to let me travel as freely as the other kids did, and gradually her reflexive dismissal wavered, and we reached a compromise. She gave me a key to the front door and attached it to a black rope lanyard; I wore it around my neck and felt that there was barely anything left to distinguish me from adults at that point.

About a month or so into kindergarten, I rode the bus home as usual, but kept one foot in the aisle this time. I was going to use my key for the first time, and we were nearing my stop. The bus braked, and I was first to stand as I waited for the driver to let us out. I poured out of the bus with the other kids that shared my stop and could see my mom waiting for me on the porch in the distance. As I closed the gap and passed the house that sometimes transformed into an ice palace, I met Mrs. Maggie.

"Chris?"

I didn't turn and barely even noticed the voice.

"Chris! It *is* you!"

Turning to my left, I saw a thin old woman hustling across her lawn, her floral-patterned dress billowing in the warm summer air. I looked to my right and then behind me, but I was the only person in the street. She was calling to *me*. I started walking faster, but my confusion had slowed my pace, and she caught up with me with her careful but quick steps.

The woman stopped in front of me, put her hands on my shoulders, and looked steadily into my eyes. As she closed her eyes tightly and furrowed her brow, I saw beads of tears streak down her cheeks. I tried to move away, but she pulled me into her and wrapped her arms around me as tightly as she could probably manage.

"Oh, Chris. I've missed you so …"

I suppose I was scared by what she was doing, but I wasn't scared of *her*. She seemed nice, and not knowing what else to do, I dropped my lunchbox, put my right arm around her, and awkwardly rested my still mending and plaster-encased left arm on her side.

"Hey!" My mom's voice struggled against the wind as she jogged from our porch to where the woman and I stood.

My mother gently, but somewhat forcefully, wrestled me from the embrace and told me to go home. As I ran home, I could hear the woman yelling "Chris!" until I vanished into the house. Once inside, I put my backpack on the dining room table and sat down on one of its chairs.

I didn't know what had just happened or what was happening right at that moment, but my concern laid mostly on what might happen when my mom came back in. I rested my head against my hand and saw a piece of white paint that had cracked and risen just above the surface of the table. I pinched it between my fingers and peeled it away; it was the first time I vandalized that table.

When my mother came back inside the house, I couldn't quite understand what her expression signified, but she didn't seem angry, so I felt relieved. I turned in the chair and faced her.

"Who was that lady, mom?"

She smiled at me as she drew closer. "Her name is Mrs. Maggie. She lives in that house you were in front of – the white one."

"The one with all the ice?"

"That's the one."

"Is she weird?" I asked hesitantly.

"No. She's … she's just a little sick, baby."

"She thought my name was Chris. She kept calling me that over and over again."

"It's okay, sweetheart. She's a nice lady, so be nice back. But when you get off the bus, you just come straight home, okay?"

And that's exactly what I would do. The strange events of the day I met Mrs. Maggie didn't trouble me for long, and if I heard her calling for me by that same wrong name, I would just walk a little faster to my house.

About a month later, my cast was removed. Josh and I had talked about swimming in the lake since before the first time he came to my house, but my cast forbid it. I could have tried to protect my arm from the lake water by wearing the latex bag that I used for showers. I considered this; only briefly, though – that bag had failed me before. Once the cast was removed, we took to swimming in the lake immediately, taking advantage of what warm weather remained. I remember how strange and weak my atrophied arm felt as it pushed through the water that first time, and I remember thinking that I'd better not push too hard or it might just snap again.

Josh and I got to know Mrs. Maggie fairly well by swimming in the lake almost every weekend, taking a hiatus only when it became time for Mrs. Maggie's yard to freeze again. When winter had passed, and Josh and I returned to the lake in the second half of kindergarten, we still wouldn't accept Mrs. Maggie's invitations or snacks, but one afternoon she surprised us with a different kind of offer.

We had expected her to invite us inside again, but this time when we looked toward her as she called to us, we saw her throw a small package into the water like one might throw a Frisbee. Hesitantly, but mostly curiously, we swam to it. Josh and I grabbed for it at the same time and wrestled it back and forth, ripping the plastic wrapping as we struggled, and throwing the object into the water.

"What is it?" Josh asked.

"I dunno. I think we have to unfold it …"

And so we did, but even after it was fully expanded, it was still hard to identify. We moved it around in the water – turning it in different ways – when finally Josh found an inflation tube jutting out of the grey and black mass. I heard him breathe deep and watched him pour his lungs into it. When he tired, I took over, and as we tread the water, we passed the gift back and forth until it was completely filled. I folded the stopper into the tube, and we flipped our inflated present over.

It was a float – one shaped and painted like a shark.

We splashed frantically to climb onto it, but each time one of us would make progress, the other would roll the float in an attempt to mount it. As we competed, I glanced at Mrs. Maggie and saw her laughing and clapping her hands. Eventually, we decided to take turns riding it, but the float soon doubled as a mechanical bull as the swimmer would invariably move underneath the shark and push up forcefully in an effort to unbalance the rider. Through all of this, Mrs. Maggie looked on us with a smile shining on her face.

As we paddled toward where we exited the lake, we yelled a "thank you" to Mrs. Maggie, and she said that seeing how much we liked it was thanks enough. She always treated us warmly, but there was a variance in her enthusiasm that we could never anticipate or make sense of. Mrs. Maggie was always at least pleased to see us, but there were times where she was simply overjoyed that we were there, swimming just behind her house. That day was one of those days, and as we pulled ourselves out of the water, carrying the float over our heads, she called to us as she sometimes would when she was excited to see us.

"Chris! John! You're always welcome here!" There were times when we could still hear her yelling those same words as we walked back into my house; we heard her that day. But we were kids, and despite how truly nice Mrs. Maggie was, her quirks sometimes got the best of us.

As we carried our new gift up the steps to my house, I opened my front door for Josh.

"After you, John."

"Oh no. Please. After you, Chris," Josh snickered.

"Oh no. I insist. After you, John," I rebutted.

"Be my guest, Chris. After you," he returned with the cadence of some crude mixture of English royalty and American upper-class snobbery.

"Would you like to come in for some snacks, John?"

"Yes I would, Chris!"

We laughed as we walked through the doorway at the same time, leaving the float on the steps behind us. I saw my mother standing in the kitchen staring at us. She moved toward us and stopped in front of us. She spoke sharply and firmly.

"Don't you *ever* make fun of her like that again. It's not funny. Do you understand me?"

Josh and I looked at one another and then back at her and nodded. My mother smiled and went back to what she was doing, and Josh and I put it out of our minds for the remainder of the day. After Josh left with his dad, I told my mom that we weren't trying to be mean, and we never talked like that in front of Mrs. Maggie. My mom said that didn't matter; she said that it was rude to make fun of anyone whether they were around or not. When I told her that she was constantly calling us by the wrong names, and we just thought it was funny, my mom seemed to search for what she wanted to say.

"Well, sweetie, you remember how I told you Mrs. Maggie was sick?"

I nodded.

"She … Mrs. Maggie is sick … up here." She gestured to her own head with her fingers.

"But you remember how, when you had that sore throat earlier this year, sometimes you'd feel okay, but then other times you'd feel really bad? That's how it is for her too. But when Mrs. Maggie gets really sick, she gets confused. That's why she messes up you boys' names sometimes. She doesn't mean to, but sometimes she just can't remember. Do you understand?"

I nodded again. "She wants us to come in for snacks sometimes."

"I know she does, sweetie. She lives in that big house all by herself so it's okay if you talk to her when you swim in the lake. But when she invites you in, you should keep saying 'no.' Be polite, and her feelings won't get hurt. Okay?"

"But she'll be less lonely when Tom comes home though?

How long until he comes back? It seems like he's always gone."

My mom seemed to struggle, and I could see that she had become very upset. Finally, she answered me.

"Honey … Tom's not going to come home. Tom's … he's in heaven. He died years and years ago, but Mrs. Maggie doesn't remember. She gets confused and forgets, but Tom's not ever coming home; he's gone, sweetie."

I was only six years old when she told me that, and while I didn't understand it completely, I was still profoundly sad for Mrs. Maggie. I knew what it was like to miss someone – how much it hurt and tore at you. But to miss someone so much while being so sure that he'd return, never knowing or remembering just how impossible that reunion truly was – I struggled to imagine what that must be like. I wouldn't learn until very recently, however, what Mrs. Maggie's life had really been like.

I know now that Mrs. Maggie had Alzheimer's disease. Her husband Tom really had been a pilot. He flew a commercial jetliner all over the eastern United States, and this caused him to spend a great deal of time away from home. After he retired, he and Mrs. Maggie kept mostly to themselves, but every time my mom would run into one or both of them, the conversation would inevitably focus on the trips they wanted to take – if they could only find the time. Tom had discounts with the airline he had retired from, but as is so often the case, their plans were always for "someday," and that day kept getting moved further down the line.

On the evening of July 4, years before I was born, Tom came to my mom's house. He was distressed, though he tried to conceal it as he casually asked my mother if she had seen Maggie. He said that she had gone out for some chicken so that he could grill it for the holiday, but that had been almost six hours ago. My mom hadn't seen her, but said she would contact Tom immediately if she saw her or heard anything.

The police brought Mrs. Maggie home about five hours after that. She had wandered from the grocery store and walked to an apartment that she and Tom had shared thirty years before when Tom was just starting his job at the airline. When the police arrived at the apartment, Mrs. Maggie insisted that she lived there with her husband, but when they read aloud the address that was printed on her driver's license, she regained her clarity and covered her embarrassment with nervous laughter.

She wasn't hurt when the police brought her home, but Tom was destroyed. He would tell my mom some time later that he had known for a long while that something was wrong with Maggie, but he had hoped that she would just get better somehow.

A few days after the police brought his wife home, Tom told my mother that he was planning on taking his wife to Rome – it had been a dream of hers since she was a young girl. Maggie had a collection of books about Rome and Italy at large that were all dog-eared on the pages with the places that she wanted to see. He said that pushing it back was simply not an option anymore; the doctors had told him that the windows of her lucidity would likely grow smaller as time pressed on. Tom began to cry and stammer as he touched his own head and said that he needed to take her now, while she was still *here*. He wanted her to be there, in the place of her dreams, while she still had a chance of knowing where she was.

He wanted her to remember.

They were old now, but he thought that they might still do some hiking, and to prepare, he began to exercise by walking around the neighborhood with Maggie. Physically, Maggie was in much better shape than Tom, so he had a lot of ground to cover if he wanted to keep up with her in Rome. He kept the trip a secret from her because he wanted to surprise her, and he justified the new exercise regimen by telling her that the fresh air and exercise would be good for them. They were getting on a plane in one month.

Tom was worried that he wouldn't be in good enough shape by the time they made it to Rome, so after Maggie went to bed, or before she woke up, he would leave the house and go on extra walks. My mom would see him almost every night when she sat outside on the porch. He would walk briskly through the cool night air, and as he passed our house, she would wave to him, and he would wave back and then bring the hand down to his lips with his index finger extended and pointing straight up, as if to say, "It's our little secret."

One night, about two weeks before the trip, my mom was sitting outside on the porch and saw, for the first time, Tom jogging. His posture wasn't professional, but he was really moving. She waved to him, but he either didn't see her or was too tired to wave back, because he kept jogging right by the house. She went back inside and went to bed for the night.

About an hour later, a knock on the front door jerked my mother out of sleep. She cracked the door enough to see through to the outside and saw a badge. It was a police officer. Behind him, the sky was filled with blue and red flashing lights that were so bright she had to shield her eyes as if the lights were the sun itself. Her first thought was that Maggie had gone missing again, and she was about to ask if that was the case when the officer spoke and then gestured toward her lawn. She squinted and let her eyes adjust just enough to break her heart.

Tom had collapsed and died fifty yards from his home, right in front of ours.

He had no identification, and so my mother pointed them toward Mrs. Maggie's house and offered to go over there with them, but they declined. She explained Maggie's condition, and they assured her that everything would be fine. My mom took one last look at Tom and went back inside.

Mrs. Maggie never found out about the trip her husband was planning for her; she knew he had died because his heart failed him while he was running, but she never knew that he was running for her.

Tom and Mrs. Maggie had had two sons: Chris and John. After Tom's death, Mrs. Maggie's condition continued to deteriorate. Her sons had apparently worked out payment plans with the utility companies and paid for Mrs. Maggie's water and electricity, but they would never visit her. I don't know if something happened between them, or if it was the illness, or if they just lived too far away, but they never came around. I have no idea what they looked like, but there were times when Mrs. Maggie must have thought that Josh and I looked like they did when they were children. Or maybe she just saw what some part of her mind so desperately wanted her to see, ignoring the images transmitted down her optic nerve, and just for a little while, showing her what used to be. I realize only now how lonely she must have been, and I find myself hoping that she understood why my friend and I never accepted her invitations.

But Josh and I were always friendly with her – extending our stay in the lake sometimes to keep her company and talk with her. The day Josh and I had our second discussion with Mrs. Maggie about the Balloon Project – and she retold the same joke about Tom's plane carrying our balloons away – just a few weeks before the year ended, an idea began to form between us after she mentioned that the lake might extend for hundreds of miles.

We had seen much of the woods surrounding my house, and we had explored the woods surrounding his; although we had never confirmed it ourselves, Josh had found out from his dad that the patches of trees that we played in near our houses were actually connected. When we learned of this, we were extremely excited – not for any particular reason – but knowing that we had been playing in the same woods the whole time, despite whether we were at my house or his, seemed to bring our houses even closer together. But there was still the matter of the lake and its tributary.

Mrs. Maggie had said that the lake's appendage might stretch on for hundreds of miles.

Since the woods were connected, Josh and I thought, despite Mrs. Maggie's speculation, the lake near my house might somehow connect to the creek around his, so we resolved ourselves to find out. For the last few weekends of kindergarten, our explorations intensified. When our summer vacation started, we would scout during the week and sell snow cones on the weekend. But it quickly became difficult to answer our own question. We needed a way to chart our progress. We needed a way to determine where we had been and where we were going. But we didn't have anything like that, so we had to make it ourselves.

We were going to make maps.

The plan was to make two separate maps and then combine them. We would make one map exploring the area around the creek near Josh's house, and make another following the outflow from my lake. Originally, we were going to make one map, but we realized that wasn't possible since I had started drawing the map of my area so huge that the route from his house wouldn't have fit. We didn't know anything about map-making, but we knew from our lessons with the map in the Community group that it was important to use the same scale consistently. This didn't involve any math – following our teacher's explanation of how maps were made, we would just put a little dot on the map for every few steps that we'd take.

We kept the map from the lake at my house and the map from the creek at Josh's house, and we would add to each when we stayed the night with each other. Josh was left-handed, and so he would often smudge the lines that he was drawing if he didn't have a flat surface to write on. Because of this, and since my penmanship was better anyway, I did most of the markings on both maps.

For the first couple of weeks, it went really well. We would walk through the woods along the water and pause here and there to add to the map. Our pace was slow, and we took breaks on the weekends while we operated the snow cone stand, but despite all this, it seemed like the two maps would come together any day. In reality, I am quite sure that the map was incredibly inaccurate, but we did our best. Our procedure was as complex as we could manage – when the bank curved, the line curved. On the upper left corner of each map, we drew a compass rose, but we didn't have a compass, nor did we know how to use one. We weren't even sure which direction north was, but it was on the wall map in our classroom, so we put it on our maps. We were the world's worst cartographers, but we were making progress.

The project seemed to be going so well that one afternoon I rerouted our usual path to the woods and took us to a nearby construction site in the neighborhood. From the cinderblocks, I guessed that they were going to place a house like mine on the plot, and the perimeter that was marked with pink-flagged wooden spikes seemed to say that it would be about the same size. I glanced around, and when I saw that no one but Josh and me was around, I jerked one of the spikes out of the ground; we ran back the way we had come and into the woods.

We were feeling optimistic and had decided that we must be getting close to finishing our project. In preparation, we thought to impale the earth with a stick each time we reached the end of the day's expedition; if we came upon the stick from the other direction, we would know we had joined the maps. This new strategy also sped up the process because it meant that rather than attempting to use our map to find the point at which we had last stopped – which was nearly impossible, though we ignored this fact – we could simply run through the woods until we saw our stake and extend the map from there.

Unfortunately, it wasn't long before the woods became too thick near the lake's long arm, and we were unable to proceed further. We debated trying to circumvent the barricade, but this idea forced us to accept that without the constant guidance of the water, our navigation skills were obliterated. Having reached a dead end, our interest in the maps stagnated, and we reduced our explorations significantly while we focused on how to make the snow cone stand more successful. I used the time to make a better, albeit deceptive, sign.

Just a few weeks later, however, the entire dynamic at my house changed. The weekend my "FOR STAMPS" dollar made its way back to me, my house descended into chaos. Police officers came to our door and talked to my mother and me for hours. One policeman with a thick, black mustache and a striking burn scar on his left forearm and hand had asked for my collection of Polaroids the day the dollar came back. My mother told me to always listen to the police, and so I did what he asked, but I think he could tell I was reluctant. Although he could have easily said nothing at all, the officer told me that he just wanted to borrow them so he could look at them too, and this made me feel better in a way.

After they left, I found myself suffocated with new restrictions on what I could do and where I could go, though I didn't understand why this was. My mother told me that the policeman might need to speak with me again, so I had to stay inside, but none of the police who ever came back over the next several weeks seemed to need or want to talk to me.

With the snow cone stand gone, Josh and I turned our attention back to the maps with revitalized interest, though our discussions were based on the telephone now. Every day we would call each other to talk about how we would move forward. We were still at the same impasse that caused us to largely abandon the mission almost a month before. Josh struck out on his own and attempted to expand his part of the map from his house, but he wasn't making headway alone. The project seemed to be dead in the water.

Gradually, however, my leash grew longer. One weekend, to my surprise, my mom didn't say no when I asked her if Josh could come over, and it wasn't too long after that when we were allowed to play outside again – though now I had to check in frequently. My mom bought me what was the nicest watch I had ever owned, and set about two dozen alarms on it – one every thirty minutes from sunrise to dusk. She told me that if I wasn't back between each alarm, then she would take the watch away. She said that I wouldn't need it anymore since I'd be confined to the house from that point on. I couldn't quite understand the need for such a policy, but I was only six years old, so of course I assented.

If Josh and I were just looking for recreation, this would have presented no challenge, but we had work to do. My mom's new policy meant that we couldn't stay in the woods for hours and continue to look for a new path; and every time we seemed to make some headway, my watch would beep, and we would have to run back to the house. We thought that we could just swim when we got to the cutoff in the woods, but that clearly wouldn't work since the map would get wet. Even if we could keep it dry, the pacing would be ruined, and the accuracy of the map (though there was surely little to begin with) would be compromised. We tried going faster when we were coming from Josh's house, hoping to see the pink-tasseled spike in the ground that would signify that the project was over, but we eventually ran into the same problem of the blockading forest. Then we had a brilliant idea.

We'd build a raft.

To keep debris off the road and off site, the construction company began throwing their scrap building material in The Ditch, since they no longer needed it for building. We originally conceived of a formidable ship complete with a mast and an anchor, but this quickly diminished into something more manageable. We set aside the wood and took several large and heavy pieces of Styrofoam that were backed with thick foam board. After several failed attempts to pilot these individual pieces of debris, we tied them together with rope and kite string in hopes that they wouldn't tip over in the water quite so easily. This project had to be a secret one, because we both knew that my mom wouldn't let us take a raft down the tributary, so we lugged the raft out of the ditch and hid it behind the biggest bushes we could find.

We launched our vessel a little down-water from Mrs. Maggie and waved a farewell to her as she motioned for us to come back her way. But there was no stopping us; we had less than half an hour before my watch beeped.

The raft worked very well, and while we both behaved and spoke as if the functionality of the raft was a given, I know I was a little surprised. We each had a fairly long tree branch to use as a paddle, but we found it was easier to simply push against the land under the water than it was to actually use them as intended.

When the water became too deep, we'd simply lie on our stomachs and use our hands to paddle the water, which still worked, albeit less well. The first time we had to resort to that method of propulsion, I can remember thinking that from far above it must have looked like a colossally fat man with tiny arms was out for a swim.

Because our charting had accelerated once we had begun running to the flagged stake, we hadn't realized that the impasse was actually quite a ways away. With each venture, we would be confident in our imminent arrival at the blockade, but the raft moved so slowly that it was taking much longer than expected. So we would sail for as long as we could and then dock the raft.

Each time we pulled it onto the shore, Josh would ask me how much farther it was, and I would take the map out of my pocket and count the dots from where I thought we were to where the map ended. "We are, I think, twenty-six dots from the end," I'd say. And Josh would nod thoughtfully. The next trip, we'd run through the woods directly to the raft, climb aboard, and go a little farther, and there would hopefully, but not always, be fewer dots.

We continued this well into first grade. Josh and I were assigned to different Groups that year, so since we didn't really see one another during the school day, our parents were more willing to let us play together all weekend each week. Because Josh's dad had taken on a lengthy construction job that required him to work over the weekends while his wife was on-call, staying at Josh's house would have been difficult. However, the fact that the telephone at my house had been shut off due to delinquent payments made staying at Josh's house *impossible* since my mom would have been unable to check on me. For Josh and me, my house became the nexus of our time together, and as much of that time as was possible was spent on the raft.

The intensity of the exploration had died down, but it was still fun, so we kept at it. The farther we made it into the woods, the shorter each trip had to be so that we could make it back to my house on time, but this made it more of a game to us. Our movement toward our destination was slow, but finally, at the very beginning of winter, the game became more serious once again.

We had made it to the impasse.

We wanted to proceed past it right away, but it was nearly time to be back to my house, so we dragged the raft onto the shore and rested it right next to the wooden marker, which we hadn't seen in weeks. We ran back to my house.

The next day, we hustled through the woods and made it back to the raft. It was so far into the woods that we had very little time to make adjustments to our plan on-scene, so we quickly pushed the vessel into the water and climbed aboard, oars in hand. As we negotiated our way past the woodland obstacle, we found that there was a bend in the water's trajectory that we hadn't been able to perceive before.

Scanning our eyes over the edge of the forest, we saw how vast and dense the woods really were in this spot. We realized that we wouldn't be able to overtake this stretch of woods after all, and so we simply stopped paddling. While we sat there on our raft, gently rocking on the calm water, I carefully looked ahead and slowly added to the map, stopping only when I had no more points to plot because the rest lay out of sight, obscured by the curving of the tributary. This felt like cheating, since we hadn't actually traveled to the dots that I was making, but we had waited so long to reach this point that I felt that I had to take advantage of it.

Before too long, we had to push back in the other direction. The woods were simply too thick, and the nearly two foot rise of earth over the tributary that exposed the twisting and damp roots of the trees above meant that there was no place to dock our vessel. Disappointed, we left the raft at the same thick of trees that prompted us to build it in the first place.

Over the course of the next week, we formulated a plan. The phone at my house had been disconnected again that week for missed payments, so the scheming was done piecemeal while waiting for the bus to pull up after school. By the time Josh got to my house the following weekend, I had already completed my part of the mission; I looked at him and attempted to discern if he had come prepared as well. My mother told us that if we were going to go outside, we needed to hurry up; she was cooking dinner, and by the time we got done eating, it would be too late to go back out. We left straight away.

"Did you do it?" he asked.

"Yeah, are you ready?"

"Yeah."

We disappeared into the trees.

Just two days before, I had gone outside to play. Rather than running into the woods, I grabbed the shark float and stealthily carried it to the side of the house. As quickly as I could, I deflated it and rolled it up. Having not considered what I would actually do with it once it had been transformed, I snuck my way to the crawlspace and pried the gateway open just enough to push the now tubular float inside. A little while later, I retrieved it, and as fast as I could, ran into the woods and to the blockade. I tried to inflate the float as I moved, but after tripping over it twice, I abandoned the multitasking and waited until I had reached my destination to finish the job.

When Josh and I reached the site, however, our plan seemed to unravel.

"I thought you said you brought the float!"

"I did … I—"

"Then where is it?!" Josh roared. He was already disrobing, revealing the bathing suit that he had put on under his shorts.

"I wedged it between the raft and the tree! I even tied it to the tree with a triple-knot."

"Well it must have blown away!"

That didn't make sense. I had kicked the float hard just before I ran back to my house, because I wanted to make sure it was secure; it hadn't budged even an inch. As I looked around the area hoping to see the float, a strange feeling began to grow inside me. Something was off, but I wasn't immediately sure what it was. The realization struck me hard and fast.

"What about the towel though?"

"What towel?" Josh returned.

"I brought a towel for you, just like we planned. I set it right under the corner of the raft … do you think it blew away too?"

"It doesn't matter now anyway. Let's just go back."

And so we did. We had planned for Josh to use the float to help him swim out past the blockade. It was getting too cold for us to leave the house in our swimsuits with my mother's approval, so he had to sneak the suit, just as I had snuck the float. He wouldn't have been able to chart his journey on the map, but if he made it to the end, then at least we would have had some idea of how far it extended. This was our trump card, so to speak; it was our last way of making any real progress, and it had been ruined. It started to seem as if we would never finish the map.

But then, finally, we caught a break.

On a Saturday evening, around seven o'clock, Josh and I were eating microwave dinners when one of my mom's coworkers knocked on our door. Her name was Samantha, and I remember her vividly now because, employing what I had learned from watching movies, I would propose to her a couple of years later when my mother brought me to work with her to pick up her paycheck; Samantha would tell me that I was sweet, but maybe we should wait until I was a bit older.

Samantha began talking to my mother, and as she did, her gaze became fixed upon Josh and me. She paused for a moment, laughed, and said, "Wow! They really do look alike! You weren't kidding." I had heard my mother say this about us before, but I didn't see it.

My mother corralled her coworker's attention and listened to the rest of what Samantha had to say. After a moment, my mom told Josh and me that we had to go to work with her so she could fix a problem that had arisen. She said that it would take about two hours, and I gathered that the problem was Samantha's fault and discussing it in the car was why it wouldn't take more time.

We all walked out of the house. My mom seemed apprehensive about bringing us to where she worked; once, when she couldn't find a babysitter, her boss had formally reprimanded her for bringing me in with her for the day. I opened the rear door of my mother's car and was just about to climb in when I heard her yell.

"Shit!"

I flinched and stepped down onto the concrete driveway.

My mom was leaning over, looking at the deflated front passenger-side tire. The sunlight was fading, and she struggled to survey the damage.

"What's wrong?" Samantha called, as she stood behind her opened car door.

"There's a fucking nail in my tire."

She muttered some other profanities and cursed the construction workers that had left their mess in the road, as she ushered us to Samantha's car. She paused when she opened the back door. There were no backseats.

"Are you fucking kidding, Samantha?"

"I'm having the cushions replaced and reupholstered …"

After fuming for a moment, she took Josh and me back up to the house and walked us inside. She seemed flustered, but she was still stern as she leaned down in front of us and alternated locking her eyes onto me and then Josh. She said that under no circumstances were we to leave the house or open the door for anyone. There would be a call every half-hour from her when she got to work in order to check in on us. She asked if we understood, and we nodded. She looked me dead in the eye as she was closing the door and said, "Stay put."

As soon as she closed the door, I walked to the kitchen, took the phone off the base, and held it to my ear.

Nothing.

Our phone was still disconnected from having not paid the bill, and Josh and I knew this because we had asked my mom to order us a pizza only a couple hours before. She had snapped at me about the phone and told us we could have frozen dinners. She must have forgotten in all the confusion, and I realize now that must have been why Samantha had come by unannounced. Of course, we had no way of knowing whether the phone might be turned back on at any moment, but that thought didn't even cross our minds.

This was our chance.

We watched my mother and Samantha drive down the serpentine road toward the exit, and as soon as the car rounded the last visible bend, we ran to my room. I dumped my backpack out while Josh grabbed the map.

"Hey, do you have a flashlight?" Josh asked.

"No, but we'll be back way before dark."

"I was thinking that we should have one, just in case."

"Well, I don't know where one is … Wait!"

I ran into my closet and pulled a box down from the top shelf.

"You have a flashlight in there?" Josh asked.

"Just hold on!"

I opened the box and revealed three Roman candles that I had taken from the pile amassed for July Fourth that past summer, along with a lighter that I had managed to take from my mother some months before. These things would ensure that we at least had *some* light if we needed it. Neither of us was afraid of the dark, and this was a little bit before I had been given an opportunity to be truly afraid of these woods at night, so it wasn't fear that motivated our search for a light source – only practicality. We threw it all in my backpack and bolted out the backdoor, making sure to close it so that Boxes wouldn't get out. We had one hour and fifty minutes.

We ran through the woods as fast as we could and made it to the raft in about fifteen minutes. We had our bathing suits on under our clothes, so we stripped off our shirts and shorts and left them in two separate piles about four feet from the edge of the water. We untied the raft from the tree, grabbed our branch-oars, and cast off.

This was it.

We tried to move rapidly to reach a point beyond the contents of our ever-expanding map, as we didn't have time to waste seeing old sights. We knew that we were slower in the raft than on land, and that we would be in the raft for quite a while after the cutoff since the woods were too thick to walk through. This meant that we'd have to ride the raft back to the original docking site, even if we found a new place to dock it further ahead.

After we passed the last charted part of our map, the water began to get so deep that we found that we could no longer touch the bottom with our tree branches, so we lay on our stomachs with the branches under our chests from left to right and paddled with our hands. The sun was dropping below the canopy, and as a result, it was becoming harder to distinguish the trees from one another. I think we were both too excited to notice how quickly the light was fading.

As the sun retreated more, we paddled faster with our arms; the noise of our hands repeatedly confronting and breaking through the water's surface tension was loud, but not loud enough to completely overpower the sound of the crunching of dead leaves and the snapping of fallen sticks in the woods to our right. As we would slow our pace and quiet our actions, the rustling in the woods would seem to cease, and I began to wonder if it was really ever there at all. We didn't know what kinds of animals resided this far into the woods, but I was confident that we didn't wish to find out.

As I amended the map that Josh was illuminating with the lighter, we were suddenly confronted with the fact that the sounds were not imagined. Rapidly and rhythmically, we heard the woods speak out.

crunch

snap

crunch

It seemed to be moving slightly away from us, pushing through the woods just beyond our map. It had become too dark to see. We had misjudged how long the sun would linger.

Nervously, I called out.

"Hello?"

There was a brief moment of breathless tension as we lay static in the water; the only sound was that of the water gently rolling against the side of our raft. This silence was suddenly broken by laughter.

"'*Hello*?'" Josh cackled.

"So what?"

"Hello, Mr. Monster-in-the-woods. I know you're sneaking around, but maybe you'll answer to my 'hello'? Helloooooo!"

I realized how stupid it was. Whatever animal it was, it wouldn't respond. I hadn't even realized I'd said it until afterwards, but if anything was actually there, I obviously wouldn't get a reply.

Josh continued. "Helloooooo," in a high falsetto.

"Helloooo," I countered with as deep a baritone as I could manage.

"'Ello there, mate!"

"Hel-lo. Beep boop. We are robots."

"hhheeeEEELLLLLOOOoooo"

We continued mocking each other with increasingly elaborate salutations, while we dug our arms into the water and moved them in a counterclockwise direction so we could turn the raft back the way we had come. When the front of our raft had pivoted enough that it faced the seemingly impenetrable woods, a sound floated out from them that chilled my blood so much that the winter water just below might have felt temperate.

hello

It was a breathy and airy whisper, the kind you might hear as someone read to himself – broadcasting his voice but not realizing it. It had come from a spot just off the map, which now sat behind us as we slowly drifted away back toward charted territory. Josh and I looked at one another; I could read the fear on my friend's face, and any hope that I had been fooled by my imagination disappeared. All options seemed equal in their futility; we were too slow on the raft to outpace anything. We would be so much faster on land, but we had no feasible way to get onto it, though that was the last place we wanted to be at that moment. I shifted on the raft and faced the direction of the sound as I fumbled with the Roman candle. I wanted to see.

"What're you doing?!" Josh hissed.

But I had already lit it. As the sparking fuse sank into the wrapper, I held it toward the sky. I had never actually shot one of these myself; I thought to just use it like a flare in the movies. A glowing green orb rocketed out toward the stars and then quickly extinguished. I lowered my arm more toward the horizon; I could remember that there were several colors, but I couldn't remember how many times one of these fired before being depleted. A second ball of red light burst out and fizzled above the trees, but I still saw nothing.

"Let's just go!" Josh pressed, as he turned back toward the direction from which we had come and began paddling desperately.

"Just one more …"

Lowering my arm directly at the woods in front of me, another red ball of fire was launched from my paper cannon. It traveled straight ahead until it collided with a tree, briefly exploding the light in a much greater diameter.

Still nothing.

I dropped the firework in the water and watched as one more struggling fireball burst free, only to die quickly, drowned by the water. Doubt had already started to sink into my mind as we began paddling in the direction of my house. Suddenly, a loud and unconcealed rustling in the woods restored my certainty. The breaking of branches and the trampling of fallen leaves overpowered the sound of our splashing.

It was running in the same direction we were pointed.

"C'mon, man! Paddle!" Josh commanded.

We were thrashing frantically in an effort to increase our speed. Reflexively, we began trying to kick our legs, which were dangling over the side of the raft, though not touching the water. In our panic, we jostled the raft too violently, and I felt one of the ropes under my chest loosen.

"Josh, be careful!"

But it was too late. Our raft was breaking. I tried to pull the rope taut, but I wasn't strong enough, and Josh began drifting away. I reached for his hand, but not quickly enough. We each held onto a separate piece of Styrofoam, but we knew individual pieces wouldn't suffice from when we had first built the raft. We bobbed and rocked as our legs dangled beneath us in the cold water.

"Josh! Quick!" I yelled as I pointed at the water right next to him.

He scrambled, but it was too cold to move quickly, and we both watched as the map floated away.

"W-wha-a-at do we d-do now?" Josh chattered.

It was cold. We needed to get out of the water. Swimming directly back wasn't an option, and we couldn't go back into our woods – there were greater problems than the congestion of trees now. I turned my eyes to the other side of the tributary and the woods that bordered it. We had never even thought of going into those trees before – we just didn't consider them part of our woods. They would have to be now, though.

"This w-w-ay." I began kicking my stiff legs in the water, and Josh followed. We propelled ourselves to the opposite shore.

The woods were just as thick on this side of the tributary, but we had no real choice. We abandoned what remained of our raft and clawed our way out of the water and into the alien woods as the sun took its final bow somewhere on the western horizon.

Taking care with each step, we marched through the trees and stayed close enough to the water so we could see where we needed to cross when we got there. Our breath steamed in the cool air, and every now and then, a violent shiver would quake through my still-soaked body. We were taking care not to make too much noise, but apparently so was the source of the voice that had greeted us earlier, because our footsteps were the only sounds.

Suddenly, the sound of a cracking branch echoed somewhere in the distance. Josh and I stopped and held each other's gaze. Too afraid to talk, Josh mouthed the words, "What do we do?" I shook my head and brought my finger to my mouth, telling him to keep quiet while we listened. Every part of me was screaming to run, except for the one that was too scared to do anything at all, and so we just stood there.

There was another cracking limb. I held my breath.

It was answered by the sound of dead leaves being crushed. I looked at Josh and could barely see his tears through my own.

crunch

...

snap

...

crunch

snap

snapsnapcrunchsnapcrunch

No. He's running! I thought I had said this aloud, but I suppose I actually hadn't, because Josh yelled to me as I ran furiously away from the stampeding sound behind us.

We were running fast, but not fast enough; the sound was getting closer. We leapt over decaying trees and tore through thorn bushes. The sound was just behind us now. There was no way we could outrun it – it would overtake us any second. I wanted to look back, but I forced myself to stare ahead. "Josh, the woods!" I yelled. Just ahead, the trees were tangled in a gnarled mass that would be too thick to run through. Should we dive into the water? Could we charge through the dense woods in front of us? Josh didn't say anything. He seemed at as much of a loss as I was. In a flash, Josh grabbed my arm and pulled me behind a large oak tree. We stood there like statues.

The sound stopped.

Steam billowed out of our mouths and into the frosty air as we tried to catch our breaths. I covered my mouth with my hand to conceal the blasts of visible air, and I motioned to Josh to do the same. There was a rustling behind us. I leaned my back against the tree to steady my shaking legs so my feet wouldn't audibly grind the leaves under them. We tried to be as quiet as possible.

We waited, shivering against the tree and sensitive to the sound of every movement behind us. Perhaps it was too dark for our pursuer to see where we had hidden. Perhaps if we quietly stood there for long enough, it would be over.

beepbeep! ... beepbeep! ... beepbeep!

My watch!

The last alarm for the day was sounding. I smashed my fingers on the buttons, but the cold had numbed my hands, and fear had clouded my mind. I couldn't remember how to stop it. Hundreds of times ... I had silenced that alarm hundreds of times, but there I stood fumbling and trembling, unable to end its high-pitched death knell.

"Stop it!" Josh pleaded.

"I'm trying ..." I whimpered.

The rustling behind us began to move. It was getting closer now. I tore at my wrist and yanked at the plastic clasp and rubber band until it finally came off. With a whipping of my arm, the watch landed and sunk into the water.

But it was too late; the crunching and snapping was right next to us now. We had nowhere to run anymore. I closed my eyes tightly, squeezing tears out of them, which rolled down my face. Defeated and terrified, I collapsed at the base of the tree and wrapped my arms around my knees, pressing them to my chest. A figure appeared in my peripheral – emerging from its hiding spot on the side of the same tree that we had hoped would conceal us. I turned my head so my eyes could take it in.

It was a deer.

I stared at it in disbelief, and it stared back at me in what might have been confusion or curiosity. It was the closest I had even been to a deer before – or since, for that matter. Even in the poor light of the pale moon, I could see the texture of its fur and the moisture on its nose.

"Get out of here!" Josh snarled in a tantrum, apathetically throwing a small stick at the creature. It bounded off into the woods; we could still hear it long after it had disappeared from sight.

We trod through the woods, moving as the dead might move. Exhausted by both fear and the winter air, we didn't speak another word until we had arrived at the point from which we had departed; only now we were on the opposite side of the water. The tributary was narrower here, but neither of us wanted to get back into the water to cross. Josh asked me what I thought we should do, but I didn't respond. I thought that if we continued through the woods along the water, we would get to the lake, and we could just circle around it. But that would take far too long. I didn't have my watch anymore, so I didn't even know what time it was; for all I knew my mother could be home already. There was no time.

"We have to cross here," I said.

As quickly as we could, we moved through the water and onto the opposite shore. The earth sloped into the water here, so we were able to simply walk out of it and back onto familiar ground. We took off our swimsuits and were desperate to get into dry clothes that would shield us from the biting chill of the air. I slid on my shorts, but there was something wrong. I turned to Josh.

"Where's my shirt?

He shrugged and gestured toward the water, "Maybe it got knocked into the water and floated into the lake?" As he motioned, I saw one of the pieces of our Styrofoam raft floating in our direction – back toward the lake.

I told Josh to go back to my house and to say that we were playing hide and seek if my mom was home. I had to try to find my shirt.

I ran behind the houses and peered out over the water while scouting along the shoreline. It occurred to me that with any luck I might find the map too – if the raft had floated this way, then maybe the map had. I was moving fast because I needed to get home, and I was about to give up when my concentration was interrupted by a sound coming from just behind me.

"Hello."

I whipped around. It was Mrs. Maggie. In the porch light, she looked incredibly frail, and the usual warmth that wrapped her manner seemed to have been snuffed out by the chill. I couldn't remember ever seeing her without a smile, and so her face looked strange to me.

"Hi, Mrs. Maggie."

"Oh! Hi, Chris!" The warmth and smile had returned to her, even if her memories had not. "I couldn't see it was you in the dark there. What're you doing out so late?"

"J-j-just playing with a friend …" Now that my rapid movements had stopped, the cold had started to creep into me again, and I could feel my teeth chatter against themselves. I was beginning to feel weak; each breeze seemed to drive the icy water on my skin through it and down to my bones.

"M-Mrs. Maggie ..." I thought for a moment and collected myself. "Mrs. Maggie, c-c-an I come inside? I just need a t-towel." My head began to swim.

"Not right now, Chris. Your ... bother, how do I put this?" She seemed to search for the words, as I half-heartedly searched for my missing shirt and any scrap of paper that might be the map. She spoke out again at the same time I did, and her voice fell dully on my ear.

"Mrs. Maggie, have you seen—"

"—om's home!"

I felt the world drop out from under me. "Mom's home!"? Had she just said that? She was still talking, but I couldn't hear her anymore. I abandoned my search immediately and ran around the side of her house. I could hear Mrs. Maggie running through her house parallel to me. My legs felt weak, but I pushed them hard against her concrete driveway. My stomach twisted when I saw my mom's car in our driveway, but then I remembered that she hadn't taken her car. I thundered down toward the street and could hear Mrs. Maggie walking briskly across her frozen yard behind me – the ice-covered grass snapping and crunching beneath her feet – but I didn't look back.

Instinctively, I ran around the house and went to the backdoor. I eased it open. I couldn't hear anything – no yelling, no talking, not a single sound. I slid into the bathroom that connected to my bedroom and cracked the door open. I heard Josh yell, and I flung the door open the rest of the way.

"You scared the crap outta me!" he protested.

"Is my mom home?"

"No."

The tightness in my stomach relaxed, and I could feel my whole body slump a little in relief. Had I heard Mrs. Maggie right? I supposed that it wasn't very surprising that she could be wrong about mom being home when she had trouble remembering what my name was. Josh had already changed his clothes and was looking much more comfortable than I felt. I went into my closet, stripped the wet clothes off, and put some dry ones on. It couldn't have been more than five minutes later that my mom came home. We'd actually gotten away with it, even though we'd lost the map.

"Couldn't find it?"

"No, I looked hard, but I didn't see it. I saw Mrs. Maggie, though. She called me Chris *again*. She's pretty scary at night."

"Don't you *ever* make fun of her like that. Understand?!" Josh whispered in a mocking tone so that my mom wouldn't overhear.

We both laughed, and he asked me if she had invited me in for a snack, joking that the snacks must be terrible since she couldn't even give them away. I told him that she hadn't – that I had actually tried to invite myself in and been rejected – and he was surprised. As I thought about it, it really was surprising. Nearly every time we had seen her, she had invited us in for snacks, and here I had invited myself, and she said no. But she had evidently thought that my mom was home, so maybe it wasn't so strange that she didn't want me to come in.

The subject turned to what had happened in the woods. We discussed it at the lowest possible volume; we were no longer sure about what we had heard. When Josh mentioned the Roman candle, it occurred to me that the lighter I had taken on the raft might still be in my pocket; even if we had gotten away with our secret mission, if my mom found a lighter in my pocket, the penalty would be severe.

The fact that I had thrown my watch into the water and would have to explain why I no longer had it was slowly presenting itself to my attention, but I subdued its nagging while I grabbed the shorts off the floor and patted my pockets. I felt something, but it wasn't the lighter. I squeezed it and felt it crinkle in my hand. From my back pocket, I removed a folded piece of paper, and my heart leapt. *The map?* I thought desperately. *But I watched it float away.* As I unfolded the paper, my palms began to sweat as I tried to understand what I was seeing.

Drawn on the paper inside of a large oval were two faceless stick figures holding hands – one much bigger than the other. The paper was torn so a part of it was missing, and there was a number written near the top right corner: either "15" or "16." I nervously handed Josh the paper and asked him if he had put it in my pocket at some point, but he scoffed at the idea. I put the question to him again, hoping he would change his answer – that he had just forgotten that he'd done it. He denied it again and asked why I was so upset. I pointed toward the smaller stick figure and what was written next to it.

It was my initials.

Josh kept talking, but I wasn't really listening anymore – my eyes were stuck on the piece of paper. I had to continuously and actively refocus my vision, which would blur as my mind meandered trying to make sense of it. I put the drawing in my collection drawer, and Josh went home the next day.

I had always attributed the odd exchange with Mrs. Maggie to her being sick – the product of a mind too young to understand and a mind too old to remember. She was such a lonely woman, and although I was too young to appreciate that fully, there must have been some part of me that did, because I never went out of my way to correct her when she called me by the wrong name.

That night was the last time I saw Mrs. Maggie. It was the last time her yard would be transformed into an arctic kingdom by her poorly timed sprinklers. But, as a kid, you just accept that people come and people go. That's just the way the world is – they have their own lives, and as they live them, sometimes that takes them out of yours. Only later do you look back and ask yourself: what happened? Where did they go?

I didn't understand why Mrs. Maggie had left. I didn't understand what I was watching weeks later when I saw men in strange, orange biohazard suits carry what I thought were black bags full of garbage out of her house, leaving the whole neighborhood blanketed in a faint but festering smell of decay. I still didn't understand when they condemned the house and boarded it up.

But I understand now. I understand that I had simply gotten the warning wrong. I thought she had tried to alert me to go because my mom was home. But that was wasn't it. I had heard what I'd been listening for, just as Mrs. Maggie had always seen what she was looking for. Had I been listening more attentively and less selfishly, had I had the capacity to recognize just how profound her confusion and loneliness really were, then maybe I would have heard the warning that she was really giving me – even though she didn't realize that it *was* a warning. She never said "Mom's home." She had told me, with an explosion of misguided joy, what could only be meaningful to me now that I can't do anything that would truly matter.

Those men weren't carrying garbage in those bags. I am as certain of that as I am of what Mrs. Maggie said that night and who had really come home, regardless of what name she called him.

That night, she told me, "Tom's home."

||||

SCREENS

At the end of the summer between kindergarten and first grade, I caught the stomach flu. The sickest I had ever been up to that point was the week in kindergarten that I had been stricken with a sore throat, but the stomach flu was an entirely different challenge. It has all of the components of the regular flu; however, with the stomach flu, you throw up into a bucket and not the toilet because you are sitting on it – the sickness gets purged from both ends. I stayed in bed for almost ten days, and just as it seemed that my body had fought the plague into submission, it was granted an extension, albeit in a different form.

One morning, just a day or two before school resumed, I woke up and began to panic, thinking for a moment that I had gone blind. My eyelids were so fused together by the dried mucus generated during the night that I couldn't open them – I had to pry my eyelids apart with my fingers. I had pinkeye.

When I started first grade, it was with a kink in my neck, caused by more than a week of bed-rest, and two swollen, blood-shot eyes. Either of these things individually might have been manageable, but as I walked through the door and into the school, there was a noticeable quieting in my peers' chatter as they looked at my infected eyes and awkward, hunched comportment.

Josh had been assigned to another Group, which I had known about for weeks, but eating schedules weren't determined that far in advance. It wasn't until my class was brought to the lunchroom that I discovered that Josh had also been assigned to a different eating period. So, due to my afflic-tion and the absence of my tablemate, in a cafeteria bursting with two hundred kids, I still had a table all to myself.

It's a bit poetic that it is so easy to take advantage of those who have no advantages to begin with. After the first several days of first grade, I started bringing spare food in my back-pack that I would take into the bathroom to eat after lunch, since my school meals were usually confiscated by older kids who knew that I wouldn't stand up to them since no one would stand with me.

This dynamic persisted even after my condition cleared up since no one wants to be friends with the kid who gets bullied, lest they have some of that aggression directed toward them-selves. There's an expression that says "you have to have money to make money," and while friendship itself is surely priceless, making friends seems to operate by the same rules. The fact that I was relatively personable in class did little to counter the fact that most of my classmates recognized me as the kid who sat alone at lunch. I was unable to make friends in class because I was unable to make friends at lunch, and the opposite held true as well; this loop fed itself for weeks.

In kindergarten, most of my peers had grouped-off with several friends, rather than pairing-off with only one, like I had. This meant that in first grade it would have been difficult to insert myself into their fold, even if I hadn't been a leper. With no friends, my ability to make any was jeopardized, and as the bullying grew more frequent, potential acquaintances grew more distant.

I came to dread going to school in the morning, to the point that there was more than one occasion where I cried when my alarm clock signaled the start of my day. My only reprieve was waiting for the school bus with Josh in the afternoon so that we could discuss our continued navigation of the tributary, but this simply wasn't enough to make the rest of the days bearable. Finally, and unexpectedly, my situation was improved by the intervention of a kid named Alex.

Alex was in the third grade, though he was bigger than most of the other kids in any grade at my school. His greater size wasn't just vertical – Alex was fairly overweight. His parents had attempted to hide their son's mass by outfitting him with oversized shirts that buttoned up the front and didn't cling to his body so easily or so tightly. However, when he sat down, the fabric would be stressed, and the openings between some of the buttons would purse, which would reveal the fat on his stomach that the baggy shirt was meant to cover. Of course, no one ever pointed this out to Alex.

Despite his intimidating size, Alex always seemed nice enough. I never saw him pick on another kid, and he didn't seem to be self-conscious about anything – one of the benefits of not having to worry about being bullied. About five minutes into lunch, sometime during the third week of school, he walked up to my table with his tray and sat down. There were several times when it looked as if he was about to say something, but they were always false starts. He left when lunch was over, and the process began anew the next day.

I was curious as to why he had suddenly decided to sit next to me, but I was hesitant to bring it up; his company had put an immediate end to the shortage of my food supply, and I would be a fool to do anything to jeopardize this new relationship. Ignoring my curiosity, I tried to strike up a conversation with him several times, but he would only ever respond with enough effort to close whatever subject I had broached. I had never spoken with him at length, and so I was having difficulty determining whether he was distracted by something in his thoughts or if he was simply slow. He wasn't being rude in his curt replies, but they left no room for an actual dialog to develop.

Against my better judgment, I confronted him on the third day he sat across from me silently eating his lunch. He seemed at a loss initially, not because he didn't know the answer, but because he knew I would ask but had not yet thought of how he would respond. After fumbling and stammering for a moment, he simply blurted it out.

He had a crush on Josh's sister, Veronica.

Veronica was in fourth grade and was probably the pretti-est girl in the school. Even as a six-year-old who fully endorsed the notion that girls were disgusting, I still knew how pretty Veronica was. When she was in third grade, Josh told me, two boys had actually gotten into a physical fight because of her; it erupted out of an argument concerning the significance of the messages she had written in their yearbooks. One of the boys eventually hit the other in the forehead with the corner of one of the yearbooks, and the wound required stitches to close. While not one of those two boys, Alex, too, wanted her to like him and confessed that he knew that Josh and I were best friends.

Although he had difficulty articulating it, probably because it was an embarrassing request, I gathered that he had hoped that I would convey his ostensibly philanthropic deed to Veronica, and that she would presumably be so moved by his selflessness, that she'd take an interest in him. If I talked him up to Veronica, he would continue to sit with me for as long as I needed him to.

Because this was during the time when Josh mostly stayed at my house navigating the tributary with me, I didn't have the chance to bring it up to Veronica, because I simply didn't see her. Even if I had, I'm not sure what I could have said that would have worked in his favor, aside from simply saying that he was a nice guy. But I needed to convey the message. It seemed like Alex had taken a liking to me and might continue to sit with me regardless of whether I held up my end of the agreement, but whether or not he realized it, he had done me a tremendous favor, and I wanted to return it.

I told Josh about the situation, but he just made fun of Alex. Part of me understood why Josh found it funny, but I insisted that he talk to Veronica since Alex had done a nice thing for me. He told me that he would tell his sister because I wanted him to, though I doubted that he would. Josh was annoyed that people seemed to be so taken with his sister. I remember him calling her an ugly crow. I never said anything to Josh, but I remember wanting to say, even then, that Veronica was pretty and would one day be beautiful.

I was right.

When I was fourteen, I was a freshman at a high school that was comprised of two distinct populations of students. The majority of the students lived in the district for that school, and they attended it as regular pupils, but there was a small percentage of the student body that commuted to the school to attend a completely separate program with a fundamentally different curriculum that was designed to prepare students for college. I was in this program.

The school was located in a predominantly poor area, and as is often the case for whatever reason, this poverty was coexistent with an underperformance of many of the school's general population. Some of these students had full-time jobs by their junior year, while others simply elected not to come to class. As a result, the school, as a whole, was a failing one. Because the collective grade of the school was an "F," its funding from the state had been significantly reduced, which meant that it became more difficult to get the necessary resources to raise the grade of the school. As a last resort out of this true "catch-22," my program was placed in the school to raise the overall grade without having to address any of the actual reasons why the school was failing to begin with.

I had hoped that the fact that my program attracted kids from all over the city would mean that Josh and I might finally attend the same school again, since it had been ten years since we were in the same class, not to mention the same school. But there was a good deal of stigma attached to attending a program like this, and so I understood why Josh apparently decided to attend his district school. Other kids from my first elementary school, however, had made different choices.

For the most part, this common origin didn't translate into easier conversation like I had expected it might. But it did allow me to befriend someone from my elementary school that I hadn't actually known that well when I was a kid, though I remembered him very distinctly.

When I saw him, I recognized him immediately; although his hair was longer than it had been back then, his face hadn't changed that much, and I could still picture him crying and pouting after our kindergarten teacher scolded him for releasing his balloon too early.

It was Chris.

He had apparently forgotten about that episode, and when I brought it up, he attempted to deny it coolly, but laughed so hard that he completely confirmed it. The memory of him clutching the empty air with his tight fist held just out of the frame of the class photograph catalyzed a fit of laughter in the both of us. I got to know him and his friends Ryan and Adam fairly well. We didn't have that much in common, in the end, but we had similar senses of humor, and we all liked movies – and that was enough.

As a result of our one common interest, we had taken to frequenting special screenings of old movies at a place we had come to call "The Dirt Theatre." It was probably nice at some point, but time and neglect had weathered the place severely. I'm not sure if the building was built as a theatre or if it had been repurposed. The floors were level, and rather than rows of fixed seats, there were movable tables and chairs. This latter fact was actually the attempted selling point of the business – their portable furniture was featured in every commercial and advertisement.

The interior layout was so bad that when the theatre was even partially full, there were very few places you could sit and see the whole screen. In some of the theatres, there were actually support columns in the middle of the room that blocked entire portions of the screen if you were unlucky enough to sit anywhere behind them.

Despite all this, the theatre was still open, and I imagine that there were three reasons for this: 1) the tickets and concessions were cheap; 2) they showed a different cult movie on Friday and Saturday twice a month at midnight; and 3) they sold beer to underage kids during the midnight showings. I went for the first two.

The theatre showed movies during the day – ones that had

just left real theatres – and as near as I could tell, the day showings accounted for the majority of The Dirt Theatre's business.
But in all the times that I had gone to see a matinee there, not
once had a movie ever started on time. In fact, there had been a
time when the movie had started twenty minutes late, and the
projectionist had actually sped up the film so that the sched-
ule wouldn't be compromised. Despite all this, the midnight
showings *always* started at exactly midnight. It was a strange
business model, but one that must have worked because, as far
as I know, the theatre is still open for business.

In my sophomore year of high school, when I was fifteen,
Chris, Adam, Ryan, and I went to The Dirt Theatre to see
Scanners by David Cronenberg for a dollar. We had arrived
with enough time to secure virtually whatever seats we wanted,
but we sat in the very back of the theatre. I wanted to sit closer
to the front for a good view, but since Ryan had driven us, the
choice was his; rather than a good view, we were left with virtually no view at all, but for some reason Adam and I were the
only ones who seemed bothered by this.

There were no previews before the midnight feature, so
much of the audience would slide in close to show time. Just a
few minutes before the movie started, a group of attractive girls
walked into the steadily-filling theatre . Whatever conversation
my friends and I were having stalled and quickly died away as
we watched them make their way to the seats they had chosen.
Chris and the other two in our party made unsavory comments
while I sat silently and watched the girls continue on their path.
Each of the girls was attractive in her own way, but whatever

beauty the other girls might have had, it was eclipsed by the girl with the dirty blonde hair – even though I had only caught a glimpse of her profile. As she turned to move her seat, I caught a full view of her face, and it gave me the feeling of butterflies in my stomach. It was Veronica.

I hadn't seen her in a long time. Josh and I saw progressively less of one another after we snuck out to my old house that night when we were ten, and usually when I would visit him, she'd be out with friends. But here she was. Of all the places she could have been, she was sitting right in front of me at the worst movie theatre in the city. I couldn't stop looking at her. While everyone stared at the screen, I stared at Veronica – only looking away when the feeling that I was being a creep overcame me, but that feeling would quickly subside, and my eyes would return to her. She really was beautiful, just like I had thought she'd be when I was a kid.

When the credits started to roll, my friends got up and left the room; there was only one exit, and they didn't want to be trapped waiting for the crowd to clear. I lingered in hopes of catching Veronica's attention, though I had no idea what I should say. As she and her friends walked by, I took a chance.

"Hey, Veronica?"

She turned toward me, looking a little startled.

"Yeah?"

I got out of my seat and stepped a little into the light that was coming in through the open door.

"It's me. Josh's old friend from way back … How … How've you been?"

Her mind seemed to search for the right frame of reference, until finally, it clicked.

"Oh my god! Hey! It's been so long!" She motioned to her friends that she'd be out in a second.

"Yeah, a few years at least! Not since the last time I stayed over with Josh ... How's he doing, anyway?"

"Oh, that's right. I remember all you guys' games. Do you still play Ninja Turtles with your friends?"

She laughed a little, and I blushed.

"No. I'm not a kid anymore ... Me and my friends play X-Men now." I was really hoping she'd laugh.

She did. "Haha! You're cute. Do you come to these movies every time?"

What did she say?
Does she really think I'm cute?
Did she just mean I'm funny?
Does she think I'm attractive?

I was still reeling from what she said when I suddenly realized that she had asked me a question; my mind grasped for what it was.

"Yeah!" I said much too loudly. "Yeah, I try to anyway ... what about you?"

"I come every now and then. My boyfriend didn't like these movies, but we just broke up, so I plan on coming more often."

I felt my heart flutter a bit, and I tried to be casual, but I failed. "Oh, well that's cool ... not that you guys broke up! I just meant that you'd be able to come more often."

She laughed again.

I tried to recover, "So are you coming the week after next? They're supposed to show *Day of the Dead* ..."

She looked a little hesitant, so I pressed further and pretended to be charming. "I think we've gotten to know each other pretty well in the last few minutes; I'm pretty positive you'd like the movie, especially if you went to the Saturday showing."

She chuckled. "Well in that case, I'll be here!"

I wanted so badly to know if she was coming because I had asked her or if she had already intended to attend, but I convinced myself that it didn't matter; she would be there either way. I was about to suggest that maybe we could sit together when she quickly closed the space between us and hugged me.

"It was really good to see you," she said with her arms around me.

I was trying to think of what to say when I realized that my biggest problem was that I had forgotten how to talk. Luckily, Chris, who I could hear approaching from the hallway, came in and spoke for me while Veronica incapacitated me with her embrace.

"Dude. You know the movie's over right? Let's get the fuck outtu— OHHH BABY!"

Veronica let go and said that she'd see me next time. She was played out of the room by the porn music Chris was making with his mouth. I was furious, but it dissipated as soon as I heard Veronica laughing in the lobby.

On the ride home, Adam asked me how I knew the girl. I explained that he was my best friend's sister, and this caused an immediate uproar. Chris might have remembered Josh, but their reaction made me glad that I hadn't mentioned who my friend was, since that would have only served to intensify Chris' gibing disapproval. I attempted to defend myself by saying that we weren't really good friends anymore since we hardly ever spoke, but as soon as I said this, I felt terrible. There was a lull in the conversation; I think they understood that it had gone in a bad direction for me – Chris attempted to fix this by leaning over the center console of the car and making kissing sounds at Ryan. The tension broke, and my feelings of guilt began to evaporate as my thoughts returned to Veronica.

I spent the next week and a half in impatient anticipation for what I was planning on considering my first date, even though it probably wouldn't be a date at all. I thought about what I would say, whether I would try to sit next to her, and what might happen if we somehow wound up alone together, without our respective groups of friends; I even thought about what I would wear, which was not something I had ever really put much consideration into. *Day of the Dead* couldn't come soon enough.

Just a few days before the movie, however, the whole plan began to unravel. Ryan told me that he and his family were going out of town, so he wouldn't be able to drive us. Neither Chris nor Adam had cars, so as a last resort I asked my mom if she could take me. I felt nervous as I walked into the living room to ask her because she seemed to strongly prefer that I go out with a group of friends if I was going to go out at all. However, I think the real reason I was nervous was that this would leave me without any kind of buffer between Veronica and myself. No buffer except for the one offered by her friends, but that provided no comfort to me – talking to one girl made me nervous enough.

When I asked my mother, she responded by telling me that she would think about it, but I persisted, and she noticed the desperation in my voice. She asked why I wanted to go so badly since I had seen the movie before, and I hesitated before saying that I was hoping to see a girl there. She smiled and asked playfully if she knew the girl; remembering the reactions of my friends the night I had run into Veronica, I was tempted to lie, but I thought my mom might not think it was such a big deal. I reluctantly told her that it was Veronica. The smile disappeared from her face, and she coldly said, "No." When I asked her what the problem was, she told me that I should keep nagging her if my goal was to stay home all weekend, so I backed down.

Having reached an impasse, I decided that I would call Veronica to see if she could pick me up. If she said no, then at least my curiosity regarding whether she was only going to the theatre because I asked her to would be satisfied. There was still the matter of her actually picking me up at my house and how my mom would react to that, but I'd worry about that problem when it actually was a problem.

I had no idea if Veronica still lived at home, but I figured it was still worth a try. When I picked up the phone and dialed the first number, I realized that Josh might answer. I hadn't talked to him in almost three years, and if he answered, I obviously couldn't ask to talk to his sister. I felt guilty for calling to speak with Veronica and not Josh, and I felt even worse because, up until that moment, that phone number had always been *Josh's* number, but I hadn't even thought of him as I started dialing.

I tried to think of the last time that I had talked to Josh. For a moment, I thought that it was just a few months after my twelfth birthday, but I realized that I hadn't actually spoken with him then. I remembered that his parents had called and spoken with my mother – she told me that they were updating their address book and just wanted to confirm that we had the same number. I asked my mom if Josh had asked to speak with me, and my mom looked sad and said that he hadn't.

As I clutched the phone and held my thumb over the buttons, resentment started to build in me as a way to suffocate the guilt; Josh hadn't called me in years either, even after he insisted that he would. There was no reason to feel bad about any of this. I dialed the rest of the number that was still embedded in my muscle memory from having dialed it so often when we were children.

After several rings, someone finally picked up, and when I heard the click of the connecting call, I felt my heart rate accelerate. It wasn't Josh. I felt a mixture of both relief and disappointment – I realized in that second that I really missed Josh. After this weekend, I would call him, but this was my only chance to see if Veronica could or would take me, so I asked for her.

The person told me that I had dialed the wrong number.

I asked who I was speaking with, and she told me her name was Claire. I repeated the number back to her, and she confirmed. Claire said they must have changed their number, and I agreed. I apologized for the disturbance and hung up, and as soon as the phone was back on the receiver, I became intensely sad because now I couldn't contact Josh even if I wanted to. I felt terrible for having been afraid that he might answer the phone.

He had been my very best friend; time and distance can wreak havoc on a friendship if you let it, and we had both been complicit in the atrophying of our relationship. I felt selfish for attempting to force the blame onto Josh just to justify my desire to see his sister. I realized that the only way I could be put back in touch with him would be through Veronica, so now, not that I needed one, I had another reason to see her.

I told my mom the Friday before the movie that I was no longer concerned with going, but was hoping she could drop me off at Chris' house the next day. She had met Chris several times and was fond of him, and since she no longer had to contend with my requests to go to the movies, she relented and dropped me off the following day, just a couple of hours before the movie.

Chris didn't know about my plan until I arrived at his house that evening. After we ate dinner with his parents, we went back to his room, and I explained my intentions to him. Since Chris only lived about a half-mile away from the theatre, my plan was to walk there from his house. His family went to church early on Sundays, so his parents would go to sleep early that night. He pretended to be offended that I was using him as a part of my scheme, but it was fairly clear that he didn't care.

Initially, I was apprehensive about telling him that I didn't want him to come with me, but whether he was simply doing me a favor or was telling the truth, before I could even bring it up, he volunteered to stay behind since he had planned on chatting with a girl he met online. Chris reminded me that Veronica was a senior in high school and that I was guaranteed to make a fool of myself. He said that the walk back to his house would be even lonelier after she laughed in my face when I tried to kiss her. I told him not to electrocute himself when he tried to have sex with his computer.

I left his house at 11:15 that night.

I tried to pace myself so I'd get there just a little before the movie. I was going by myself, so I didn't want to just loiter impatiently outside of the building. On the way to the theatre, I figured that if Veronica showed up at all, it would be too lucky for us to arrive at the same time, so I debated whether I should wait outside or just go in. If I went in first, then she might not notice me when she entered the dark theatre, but the same was true for me if I waited for her and she was already inside. It also occurred to me that she would probably be with her friends again, and I needed to figure out how to insert myself into their group without being scoffed at for being too young.

The grass on the side of the road where I walked was ankle-high, and as my shoes moved against it, I could feel the occasional mist of water from that afternoon's rain curling up and colliding with my dangling hands. The sky had cleared itself of clouds in the evening, but the cool air still lingered, and this made the walk more pleasant, despite my insecurities and uncertainties.

As I was grappling with the decision of whether to wait for Veronica or go into the theatre once I got there, I noticed that the steady stream of streaking car lights that had been overtaking me had been replaced by a single, constant spotlight that refused to pass. The road wasn't illuminated by streetlights, which was why I had been walking in the grass to begin with. I was already about two feet away from the road, but thought that it might not be far enough for a nervous motorist; I stepped a little more to my right and craned my neck over my left shoulder, ready to flag the person to pass, and I heard the squeaking of old brakes as I adjusted my posture.

A car had stopped about fifteen feet behind me.

I stopped walking and turned around to face the car. All I could see were the violently bright headlights that were cutting through the otherwise stygian surroundings. I thought that it might be one of Chris' parents; maybe they had come to check in on us and seen that I was gone. It wouldn't have taken much pressing for Chris to confess. In fact, he might have done it gladly since it would be even more humorous to him if my big date had been intercepted by his mom. I took one step toward the car, and it broke its pause and started driving toward me at a slow pace.

As it passed me, I saw that it wasn't Chris' parents' car, or any car that I recognized for that matter. I tried to see the driver, but it was too hard to see inside the car at all since my pupils had shrunk when faced with the blinding headlights just moments before. They adjusted enough that I could see a tremendous crack in the back window of the car as it drove away.

"Asshole," I muttered.

After a few more minutes of walking, I laughed a little now that the urgency of the situation had passed. I could see myself doing something like that to a pedestrian. Sometimes it could be fun to scare other people – I'd often hide around corners and jump out at my mom, after all.

I timed the walk correctly and got there about ten minutes before the movie started. There wasn't a line, so I approached the ticket seller and bought a pass for myself. He was overweight and sweating so profusely that beads of perspiration were sliding off the top of his hairless scalp and down the stringy ponytail he had fashioned with the hair that still grew on the back of his head. When he handed me my ticket, it was damp.

After about a minute, I went back to the counter, slid another dollar bill through the slot, and bought a ticket for Veronica. As the employee handed me my half of the cheap raffle-tickets they used as stubs, he snorted and said that I must really like this movie to see it twice in one weekend and buy extra tickets. I walked away even more surprised that The Dirt Theatre was still in business with him handling the cash and counting it.

I had decided to wait outside until around 11:57, since that would give me time to find Veronica inside if she was already seated. As I was reconsidering the possibility that she might not show, I saw her.

She was beautiful, and she was alone.

I waved to her and walked to close the distance. She smiled and asked if my friends were already inside. I said that they weren't coming and realized that it must seem like I was trying to make this a date; I felt my palms start to sweat inside my pockets as I rubbed the already-damp tickets between my fingers and debated whether or not I should just let her buy her own now. Despite the fact that I had come alone, she didn't seem bothered, nor was she bothered when I pressed my luck further and handed her the ticket I had already bought for her. When she looked at me quizzically, I said, "Don't worry, I'm rich." She laughed, and we went inside.

I bought us one popcorn and two drinks and spent most of the movie debating whether or not I should time reaching my hand into the popcorn bag when she did so that our hands might touch. Having seen the movie already last year, I didn't pay much attention to it; instead, I donated it to Veronica in the form of sidelong looks and occasional comments. For the past two weeks, I had played out cliché scenarios in my mind wherein she would get scared and cling to me. That didn't happen, but I thought that probably never really happened anyway.

Aside from one unfortunate interruption where I had to run out of the theatre and find somewhere that would hopefully sound like Chris' house to take a call from my mom, there were no awkward moments during the movie. Veronica seemed to enjoy the film, and before I knew it, it was over. We didn't linger in the theatre, and because this was a midnight showing and the theatre was closing, we couldn't loiter in the lobby. So we walked outside.

The parking lot of the theatre was big because it connected with a mall that had gone out of business years before.

We stood and talked for a long time as the rest of the audience drove away from the theatre. Not wanting the night to be over just yet, I continued the conversation while causally walking toward the old mall, away from where I thought Veronica had parked. Since she wasn't scared during the movie, I thought to tell her a story I had heard about this mall. As I began the tale, I looked back and saw that her car wasn't the only one left in the parking lot.

The other one had a large crack in the back window.

I stood and stared at it, puzzled and unnerved.

"So there was a robbery?" Veronica said in an attempt to put me back on the story.

"Right!" I continued. I tried to put the car out of my mind as we resumed our walk and left the theatre out of sight. "Well, kinda …

"So, this mall closed like five years ago, but way back this was the place where everyone would come to hang out and shop."

"As opposed to all the other *awesome* places in this town?" she interjected, sarcastically.

"Damn right! Anyway, everyone thinks that the place just went out of business, but that's not true. What happened was that at some point the manager, or whoever, noticed that a lot of the food inventory was going missing. I don't mean like candy bars – I'm talking about whole freezers full of food. So, he put all these security cameras everywhere, ya know, to try to catch who was taking it, but the cameras never showed anything. They'd be on all night – pointed at the freezers – but in the morning, they'd open them up, and all the food would be gone, and there'd be this huge mess."

"Spooooky!" she gibed.

"Just hang on! So the owner-guy hires these two security guards to stay overnight and keep an eye out. The first couple of nights are no problem, right? No food is missing, everything's cool. But then one night, the guard hears this huge crash coming from across the empty mall, and so he runs over to see what's going on. Then he hears these screams."

The smile was disappearing from Veronica's face.

"It's his partner. But he can't tell where the screams are coming from, exactly. On the video, it's just him running back and forth, back and forth. And he's shouting something, but the cameras don't have sound, so no one knows what he's saying."

"How do you know all this, then?"

"Just a second. So, eventually the guard runs up to one of the freezers, ya know, the one behind the Chinese food place? Well, he opens it up. He takes a look inside and backs away, and then just runs out of the mall. He didn't even lock the doors.

"The owner comes back in the morning, finds his mall unlocked and no sign of the security guards. He checks the tapes, and doesn't understand what happened, but he sees who left the door unlocked. After he checks the freezer and sees the mess and the missing food, he calls the police and sends them after the guard who just ran out.

"They find him at his house, just locked in his room, shaking. They asked him what happened, but the guy won't talk.

They ask him about the food, but the guy just keeps shaking. Finally, they take him into the station for more questioning.

"The police have a theory that these two guys were involved somehow so they start really interrogating the guy, but he just won't talk. 'Where's your partner?' they ask him. 'What happened to your partner? Where'd he take the food?' But the guy won't crack. Finally, they start threatening him with jail time, and he just breaks down.

"The guy says he saw his partner being pulled through the big drain in the floor of the freezer. The police are like 'Pulled? Pulled by what?' And the guy just starts crying and screams, 'A MONSTER!'

"They do an investigation but never find the partner, but when they opened the grate on the floor of the freezer, they saw the pipe was gone, and it was just this big hole. The investigation shuts the mall down for months, and the owner goes bankrupt."

"What about the guy? The security guard?" Veronica asked, her voice trembling a little.

"He winds up in the insane asylum down south. He draws these pictures of the monster during free time, but they always look different …"

I started trying to guide us to one of the giant windows that stretched from the foundation to the roof of the mall.

"But here's the thing. They never found any monster, but they did find all kinds of boxes and big plastic wrappers in that hole under the freezer. And they found the missing guard's flashlight down there too. It was smashed to pieces."

We were right in front of the window.

"But the craziest part is that they just gave up – they just shut down the mall and locked it up forever. They say that if you're quiet, and you look for long enough, you can still see the monster walking around the mall now since no one's there to bother it. But what's weird is that everyone who's ever seen it tells a different story of what it looks like." ·

I pressed my hands in C-shapes against the window and peered through the dirty glass. Veronica followed my lead. We waited silently for almost a minute, our breath fogging against the window. Right as she was in the middle of saying that she didn't see anything, I kicked the window hard with my foot, and the whole pane vibrated.

Veronica shrieked briefly and tore away from the window, grabbing my arm as she moved back.

"You jerk!" she yelled with a smile growing on her lips.

"What?! Didn't you see it?!" I started laughing. "I'm sorry! I'm sorry!"

She playfully shoved me. I had heard that story so many times from Chris, but the window-kick was my idea. Veronica seemed to like horror movies, so I was hoping that she would appreciate the story, and I was happy that she took the joke well.

As the laughter and false hostility abated, my mind returned to the car with the cracked window. Suddenly, uneasiness turned to understanding and amusement.

That makes a lot of sense. The driver of that car works here and must have figured I was on my way to the movie, I thought. Injecting real horror into the life of a horror fan seemed like an obvious move; that was exactly what I had just done.

With things more relaxed, we continued walking around the mall and started talking about the movie we had just seen. I told her that I thought *Day of the Dead* was better than *Dawn of the Dead*, but she refused to agree. I told her about when I called her old number and about my dilemma about who would answer the phone. She didn't find it as funny as I did, but she took my phone and put her number in it. She commented that it might be the worst cell phone she'd ever seen. Her evaluation wasn't rescinded when I told her I couldn't even receive pictures on it.

"At least it plays really good music," I said. She looked at me quizzically, and handed my phone back to me. I shook the phone rhythmically, and some chip of plastic or a stray metal screw that had come lose inside the phone's casing began to rattle around inside the phone. I danced in a self-mocking fashion briefly, and then tried to call her so she'd have my number, but I had no service. I power-cycled the phone, and took advantage of the high connection I always had when it first turned on. The call went through, and I watched her cancel it.

"Hey! I was going to leave you a voicemail! I had an important message for you!"

She laughed. "Oh yeah? What was it?"

"Well, maybe I don't remember anymore … should've just let it go to voicemail."

"I messed up the settings on this thing. It never goes to voicemail; it just rings forever!"

"Yeah, your phone really sucks," I said, as I shook mine like a maraca.

We both laughed. I watched as she saved my number. We walked on.

She told me that she was graduating, but she hadn't done well in school for the past couple years, so she wasn't sure if she'd even get into college. She said that she should have gone to the magnet program that I was in, since she might be in a better spot now if she had. I told her to attach a picture of herself to the college application, and they'd pay her to go there just so they could look at her. She didn't laugh at that one, and I thought she might be offended – she might have thought I was implying that she couldn't get in based on her intelligence. I nervously glanced at her, and she was just smiling, and even in that poor light I could see that she was blushing. I wanted to hold her hand, but I didn't.

As we walked down the final side of the mall, back toward the theatre, I asked her about Josh. I had asked about him when I saw her in the theatre with her friends weeks before, but she had simply brushed it aside, and I let her because I would have talked to her about anything. This time when I asked, she told me that she didn't want to talk about it. I asked her if he was at least doing okay, and she just said, "I don't know." I figured Josh must have taken a wrong turn somewhere and started getting into trouble. I felt bad. I felt guilty.

As we approached the parking lot, I noticed that the car with the cracked back window was gone and that her car was now the only one in the parking lot. I had no idea how long it took to clean up that theatre before it closed, but as consistently dirty as that place was, I wasn't surprised that the employees had already left. Veronica asked me if I needed her to drive me back to Chris' house, and even though I really didn't need her to, I wanted her to, so I lied and said that it was a long walk and that I'd appreciate it.

I had finished my soda during the movie, and all the walking was putting pressure on my bladder. I knew that I could wait until I was back at Chris', but I had decided that I was going to try to kiss her when she dropped me off, and I didn't want this biological nagging to rush me out of the car. This would be my first kiss.

I struggled, but I could think of no ruse to conceal what I needed to do. The theatre had closed, so I only had one option. I told her that I was going to go behind the theatre to piss but that I'd be back in "two shakes." It was obvious that I thought it was hilarious, but she seemed to laugh more at how funny I found it than at how funny it clearly was.

On the way toward the theatre, I stopped and turned toward her. I told her that I had a weird question, and her interest piqued. I asked her if Josh had ever told her that some kid named Alex had done something nice for me. She paused to think for a moment and said that he had; she enquired as to why I had asked, but I said it was nothing. Josh really was a good friend.

When I went to go behind the theatre, I realized that there was a chain-link fence extending off of and running parallel to the walls of the building. She could still see me where I was standing, and the fence seemed to stretch on endlessly, so I thought I'd just hop it, duck out of sight, and return as quickly as I could. It may have been too much of an effort, but I thought it polite. I climbed the fence and walked just a little ways until I was out of sight. I heard Veronica yell for me to not stand on any grates or the mall-monster might get me.

For a moment, the only sounds were the crickets in the grass behind me and the collision of liquid and cement. Before too long, however, these sounds were overpowered by a noise that I can still hear when it is quiet and there are no other noises to distract my ears.

In the distance, I heard a faint but distinct screeching, which quickly subsided, only to be replaced with a cascade of thundering vibrations. I realized quickly enough what it was.

It was a car.

The growling of the engine got louder. And then I thought. *No. Not louder. Closer.*

The rumblings intensified. It was growing louder still. I started back toward the fence with haste, but before I could get very far at all, I heard a brief, truncated scream, and the roar of the engine terminated in a deafening thud. I started running, but after only two or three steps, I was tripped by a loose piece of stone, and I fell hard and fast onto the concrete – my head striking the corner of a bench as I fell.

I was dazed for maybe thirty seconds, but the renewed rumbling of the engine drew my senses back, and my equilibrium was restored by my adrenaline. I redoubled my efforts. I was worried that whoever had crashed the car might harass Veronica. Briefly, but forcefully, it occurred to me that we would have to call the police. My mom would be contacted because I was a minor – that wasn't how I wanted this night to end.

As I was climbing over the fence, I saw that there was still only her car in the parking lot. I didn't see any evidence of a crash. I thought that I might have misjudged its direction or proximity, but I swore I could smell the faint and fleeting aroma of burned rubber or possibly machine smoke, and this was corroborated by a metallic taste that clung to my tongue. Each of my senses was telling me that something had happened, but my eyes defiantly returned ordinary images.

As I ran toward Veronica's yellow car, I had to change my orientation to move around it. Finally, and terribly, my eyes joined my other alerted senses. I saw what the car had hit, and my legs stopped working almost completely.

It was Veronica.

Her car was sitting between us, and as I closed the distance and walked around it, she came fully into view.

Veronica's body lay twisted and crumpled on the black asphalt of the parking lot, her limbs so unnaturally contorted that she looked like a child's discarded wooden art doll that now showcased a catalog of things the human body cannot do. As I looked at her, I actually found it hard to discern whether she was lying on her back or her stomach, and my vision warped the space around her in an attempt to see a human figure again. This optical illusion made me feel sick with dizziness to the point that I had to close my eyes for a moment for fear of vomiting.

"Veronica?" I pleaded with limp, vibration-less vocal cords

– the sound nothing more than the broken whisper of a ghost.

The bone of her right shin had cut savagely through her jeans and stood erect atop a foundation of bloodstained denim. Her other leg bent out to the side twice – as if she had a second joint in her femur. I traced her figure and saw that her left arm had been dislocated at the shoulder and was wrapped so hard and forcefully around the back of her neck that her hand fell over her right breast with her fingertips nearly touching her navel.

I stepped a little closer and knelt down, gravity doing the lion's share of the work as my legs trembled.

Her head was craned back and her mouth hung widely open toward the sky, and as I looked into her half-lidded eyes, they stared absently back into mine, as lifeless and cold as a shark's. Blood was pooling around my shoe now. There was so much of it.

When you are confronted with something in the world that simply doesn't belong, your mind tries to convince itself that it is dreaming, and to that end it provides you with that distinct sense of all things moving slowly, as if through sap. In that moment, I honestly felt that I would wake up any minute.

But I didn't wake up.

I fumbled with my phone to call for help, but I had no signal. I was depressing the power button in the hopes that the signal would return when the phone was turned back on, when I saw Veronica's phone sticking out of what I thought was her front right pocket. I had no choice. Trembling, I reached for her phone and took hold of it. As I slid it out, she moved and gasped so violently for air that it seemed as if she was trying to breathe in the whole world.

This startled me so much that I staggered back and fell onto the asphalt with her phone in my hand. She was trying to adjust her body to get it into its natural position, but with every spasm and jerk of her body, I could hear the cracking and grinding of her bones. Without thinking, I scrambled over to her and put my face over hers and pleaded,

"Veronica, don't move. Don't move, okay? Just stay still. Don't move. Veronica, please just don't move."

I kept saying it, but the words started to fall apart as tears came streaming down my face. I opened her phone. It still worked. It was still on the screen where she had saved my number, and when I saw that, I felt my heart break a little. I called 911 and waited with her, telling her that she would be okay, and feeling guilty for lying to her every time I said it.

When the sound of sirens tore through the air, she seemed to become more alert. She had remained conscious since first coming to, but now more of the light was coming back into her eyes. She was breathing steadily, but it was a gurgling, labored breathing. Her brain was still protecting her from pain, though it looked as if it was finally allowing her to become aware that something was terribly wrong with her. Her eyes rolled over to mine, and her lips moved. She was struggling, but I heard her.

"Hhh … he … p … pi … picture. M … my pictu … he took it."

I didn't understand what she meant, so I said the only thing I could. "I'm so sorry, Veronica."

I rode with her in the ambulance where she finally, and mercifully, lost consciousness. The paramedics asked me several times what happened, but I could only mumble the word "car." I was staring so vacantly that one of the paramedics shined a light in my eyes in an attempt to determine if I had been injured as well. When he returned his attention to Veronica, I felt guilty that he had even had to waste his time on me.

When we arrived at the hospital, the nurses wheeled Veronica through a set of double-doors. As the paramedics rushed by me, one of them put Veronica's purse in my lap; I fidgeted with the leather strap and sat anxiously yet absently in the waiting room. The blank stare had returned to my eyes as my mind swam in every direction with no guidance or trajectory. The shouts, coughs, cries, and talking of the emergency room waiting area became a dull buzzing in my ear as I went completely numb to all things. All things but one.

A phone was vibrating in my pocket.

My pulse quickened and my throat dried as I reached my hand into my pants pocket to fish out the phone. My mother was trying to check in on me again. I had no idea how I was going to explain this to her. I wasn't worried about getting in trouble – those consequences seemed so remote and insignificant to everything now – but what combination of words could I possibly cobble together to explain all this? Between vibrations, I clasped my hand around my phone and pulled it out.

It was off.

For just a moment, I thought the call had simply stopped,

or perhaps my phone had died just then somehow. But this moment of confusion ended as soon as the vibrations began again – still in my pocket. I still had Veronica's phone, and someone was calling it. I felt my eyes begin to water, and I reached into my pocket to retrieve Veronica's phone. I looked at the screen and could see that her dad was calling her. I needed to answer it. I needed to tell him what had happened. Veronica's mom was a nurse; maybe she could help. I needed to let someone know what was going on. But every time I tried to imagine even a fragment of what I might say, my thoughts would splinter into pieces too small to reassemble.

I kept hoping the phone would just stop ringing – that the insistence that I answer it would be over. But I knew from what Veronica had told me earlier that as long as her dad kept his phone to his ear, her phone would never stop ringing. With a burning in my chest, I moved my thumb over the phone and pressed "Ignore." Relief, guilt, and shame boiled within me, and I collapsed my head onto my knees and cried.

Collecting myself, I went to the counter to see if there was any information on Veronica's condition, but not enough time had passed for there to be any news that would be good news. Before leaving the counter, I asked if I could make a call. I dialed my mom's number into the hospital phone. Looking at the clock on the wall, I saw that it was about 4:00 A.M., and I held my breath as the line sought a connection. She answered. I told her that I was fine, but that Veronica was not. She cursed at me and said she'd be right there, but I told her I wasn't leaving until Veronica was out of surgery. She said she'd come anyway.

The police entered the hospital just a little after I hung up the phone with my mother. They didn't have many questions for me, and the ones that they did have weren't met with very helpful answers. I hadn't seen the driver. I didn't get the license plate. I could only tell them that I thought that it was a brown car, but I couldn't even tell them how many doors were on it. As the police officers were walking away, I yelled to them, and they walked back over to where I was sitting. I told them that the car I was talking about had a big crack in the back window. Sensing how impotent I was feeling, one of the officers said that would be a huge help. "Don't worry. We'll find him."

My mom and I didn't speak that much when she got to the hospital. After verifying that I was unharmed, her relief transitioned into anger. I told her I was sorry for lying, and she said that we'd talk about it later. For the majority of the time that we sat together in the waiting room, there was silence between us. There didn't seem to be anything to say. I think that had we talked more in that room – if I had just told her about Boxes or the night with the raft; if she had just told me more of what she knew – I think that things would have changed. But I didn't know that any of those things mattered; they were just distant memories of strange adventures to me. So we sat there in silence, and she looked at me while I looked at the floor. She told me that she loved me and that I could call her whenever I wanted her to come get me.

As my mom was leaving, Veronica's parents rushed in with the wide eyes of people who are attempting to see what is important in a room as quickly as possible. My mom must have called them after I had spoken with her. Veronica's dad and my mom exchanged a few words that appeared to be quite serious, while Veronica's mother talked to the person at the desk. Her mother was a nurse, but didn't work at this hospital. I'm sure that she had tried to get Veronica transferred, but her condition was prohibitive.

While all of these conversations were taking place, I slipped Veronica's phone back in her purse to hide the evidence of the conversation that I was too much of a coward to have. The police talked to each of us, including me for a second time – I told them what happened again, they made some more notes, and then they left.

Veronica came out of surgery several hours later with a thick, white cast covering 90% of her body. Her right arm was free, but the rest of her was cocooned in plaster. Her parents and I walked to Veronica's room; they never asked me for her purse, so I just set it on the table to the right of her bed. She was still under the anesthetic, but I remembered how I felt when I had my cast before kindergarten. I asked a nurse for a marker, but I couldn't think of anything to write. I slept in a chair in the corner, and went home the next day.

I came back every afternoon for several days. At some point, they had moved another patient into her room and set up a screen around both beds to act as a partition. The divider was always closed, so I could never tell if the person in the adjacent bed was sleeping; however, I once caught a glimpse and saw that in addition to the cast on his left wrist, the occupant's face was completely covered in bandages, so I decided to always speak in hushed tones just in case.

Veronica didn't seem to be feeling better, but she had more moments of lucidity. But even during these periods, we wouldn't really talk. Her jaw had been broken by the car, so the doctors had wired it shut. I sat with her for a while, but there was nothing much I could say. I got up, walked over to her, and kissed her on the forehead. As I turned to leave the room, she whispered through her clenched teeth,

"Josh …"

This surprised me a little, but I looked at her and said, "Has he not come to see you?"

"No …"

I grew infuriated. *Even if Josh had gone down the wrong path at some point, he should still come see his* sister, I thought.

I was about to express this when she said, "No … Josh … he ran away … I should've told you."

I felt my blood turn to ice.

"When? When did this happen?"

"Two years ago. A little after his thirteenth birthday."

"How … Why do you think he ran away?"

"The note … on his pillow …"

She started crying and I followed her, but I think now we were crying for different reasons, even if I didn't fully realize it. There was still so much that I didn't remember – so many connections I hadn't yet made – but I remembered the letter, even if I didn't know what it had truly meant. I told her that I had to go but that she could text me any time; I pulled the phone out of her purse and set it on the table right next to her free hand. I asked her if she was going to be okay alone, and she told me that her mom was coming in a little later that day, so she would be fine.

I got a text message from her the next day, and I hesitated before opening it. When I read it, I wished that I had hesitated just a little bit longer. It said, "Please don't come back here." It took me almost a full minute to type a simple "Why not?" in reply, because my flustered brain kept directing my fingers to the wrong keys. She said that she didn't want me to see her like that again, and I agreed begrudgingly because it was only a temporary quarantine. We texted each other every day, though I kept this from my mom because I knew that she didn't like me talking to Veronica.

The events of the night at The Dirt Theatre had caused an intense strain in the dynamic between my mother and me, and our interactions became abruptly cold and infrequent after I asked her why she hadn't told me that Josh had run away. She claimed she simply did not know; that she didn't talk to his parents anymore. In a way, I thought this made sense – if I had fallen out of touch with Josh, my best friend, then why should I expect our respective parents to stay in close contact? But the fact that she had called them before coming to the hospital meant that she had their new number, which was something that I was never privy to, and this bothered me.

Veronica's texts were generally fairly short, and mostly only in response to more lengthy texts that I would send her. I tried calling her only once; I was sure she was screening her calls, but hoped that I could at least hear her voice. She picked up but didn't say anything. I could hear how labored her breathing was; I thought I might have heard her say my name, but it was hard to tell. Eventually, I just had to hang up to stop myself from crying again.

About a week after she told me not to come see her anymore, she sent me a text that simply read,

"I love you."

I was filled with so many different emotions. No one from outside my family had ever said that to me before, and somehow reading those words – which came not as the compulsory and reflexive expression that ends phone calls between family members, but from someone who really felt it – showed me why those words were so powerful. There were so many words that I wanted to say, but only a few that I felt I needed to say:

"I love you, too."

Over the next several weeks, the intensity grew. Veronica said that she wanted to be with me, and that she couldn't wait until she could see me again. She told me that she had been released from the hospital and was convalescing at her house, but every time I asked to come see her, she would always say, "soon." In the back of my mind, a nagging guilt tore at my jubilation. I realized that her feelings for me were most likely artificial symptoms of her injuries; maybe she only felt close to me because she had almost been taken away from everything. Each time I received a message from her, however, these concerns evaporated in the heat of my happiness, and I would insist again that she let me see her.

Finally, the following week she said that she thought she might be able to make it to the next midnight movie. I couldn't believe it; I suggested that we meet somewhere that would be a little less strenuous, but she insisted that she would try. She said that she wanted to redo our date, and I admired her strength and optimism for that. I got a text from her the afternoon of the movie saying, "See you tonight."

Chris' parents had found out about everything that had happened and said I wasn't welcome at their house anymore, so I got Ryan to drive me. My mother tried to stop me, but I was bigger than her now, so I simply walked out of the house and got into Ryan's car. I explained to him that Veronica might be in bad shape, but that I really cared about her so he should give us some space. He accepted that, and we headed to the theatre.

Veronica didn't show.

I had saved a seat for her right next to me near the exit so she could get in and out easily, but fifteen minutes into *Akira*, a man slid into the chair. I whispered, "Excuse me, this seat is taken," but he didn't respond at all; he just stared ahead at the screen. I remember wanting to move because there was something wrong with the way he was breathing, but I forfeited after a while because I realized that Veronica wasn't coming, so it really didn't matter where I sat or who sat next to me.

I texted her the next day and asked if she was all right. I enquired as to why she didn't show the previous night. But she didn't respond. Despite my attempts to restrain myself and be patient, I messaged her repeatedly, pleading with her to at least tell me how she was feeling. She responded with what would turn out to be the last message I would receive from her. She simply said,

"See you again. Soon."

She was delirious, and I was worried about her. I sent her several replies reminding her about the movie and saying it was no big deal, but she just stopped replying. I grew increasingly upset over the next several days. I couldn't reach her at her home because I didn't know that number, and I wasn't even sure where they lived. However, I knew that my mom knew at least one of these things.

With no other options, I turned to my mother. I told her that I knew that she must know Veronica's parents' phone number since I suspected that she had called them the night of the accident. I told her that I needed that number. She asked why, and when I told her that I hadn't heard from Veronica in days, I felt all of what little warmth was left in her disposition dissipate.

"What do you mean?"

"I don't want to get into an argument with you over this, but she was supposed to meet me at the movies yesterday. I know there hasn't been much time since she got hit, but she said she would try to come, and after that she just stopped talking to me altogether.

"She must hate me. If we wouldn't have gone to that movie, then she would still be okay right now. I don't know what to do now. I just want to tell her that I'm sorry … that I'm sorry for everything."

She looked confused, and I could read on her face that she was trying to tell if my mind had simply broken. There was

200

intense compassion in her eyes that lingered for as long as she thought that my hold on reality had slipped. When she saw that it hadn't, this compassion dissolved into defeated tears, and she pulled me toward her to embrace me. She was beginning to sob, but it seemed too intense of a reaction to my problem, and I had no reason to think that she particularly cared for Veronica – quite the opposite seemed true. She drew in a shuddering breath, and then said something that still makes me nauseous, even now.

"Veronica's dead, sweetheart. Oh God, I thought you knew …"

I pulled away aggressively. "What? What are you talking about? She said she was doing better … She said she was feeling better, mom!"

There was a long pause.

"What happened to Veronica?!"

"She's dead, sweetie. She died on the last day you visited her. Oh honey, she died weeks ago."

She had completely broken down, but I knew it wasn't because of Veronica. I staggered backwards. This wasn't possible. *I had just exchanged messages with her yesterday.* I could only think to ask one question, and it was probably the most trivial one I could ask.

"Then why was her phone still on?"

She continued sobbing. She didn't answer.

I exploded. "Why did it take them so long to shut off her goddamned phone?!"

Her crying broke enough to mutter, "The pictures …"

My mother told me that Veronica's parents had thought that her phone had been lost in the accident, despite the fact that I had put it in her purse the night she was brought to the hospital. When they retrieved her belongings, the phone was not among them, but they didn't deactivate the line. I asked my mom why this was – why they had failed to close her account – but she said she didn't know. But I think I know. I think they just couldn't bear to do even one more thing that forced them to admit that she was gone. They probably would have kept that line active forever, but they received a call from their service provider informing them of a massive impending charge for hundreds of pictures that had been sent from her phone.

Pictures.

Pictures that were all sent to my phone. Pictures that I never got because my phone couldn't receive them. They learned that they were all sent after the night Veronica died. They deactivated the phone immediately.

I tried not to think about the contents of those pictures. But I remember wondering for some reason that I couldn't place whether I would have been in any of them.

My mouth went dry, and I felt the painful sting of despair as I thought of the last message I received from her phone …

See you again. Soon.

||||

FRIENDS

On the first day of kindergarten, my mother had elected to drive me to school; we were both nervous, and she wanted to be there with me all the way up to the moment I walked into class. It took me a bit longer to get ready in the morning due to my still-mending arm. The cast came up a couple inches past my elbow, which meant that I had to cover the entire arm with a specially designed latex bag when I showered. The bag was built to pull tight around the opening in order to seal out any water that might otherwise destroy the cast. Since I still had use of my dominant hand, I had gotten really adept at cinching the bag myself; that morning, however, perhaps due to my excitement or nervousness, I hadn't pulled the strap tight enough, and halfway through the shower, I could feel water pooling inside the bag around my fingers. I jumped out and tore the latex shield away, but could feel that the previously rigid plaster had become soft after absorbing the water.

Because there is no way to effectively clean the area between your body and a cast, the dead skin that would normally have fallen away merely sits there. When stirred by moisture like sweat, it emits an odor, and apparently, this odor is proportionate to the amount of moisture introduced, because soon after I began attempting to dry it, I was struck by the powerful stench of rot. As I continued to rub it frantically with the towel, the cast began to disintegrate into thick white strips that rained down upon my feet while small white flakes wafted into the air and seemed to hover like snowflakes.

I was growing increasingly distressed – I had put as much effort as a child could into his very first day of school. I had sat with my mom picking out my clothes the night before; I had spent a great deal of time picking out my backpack; and I had become exceedingly excited to show everyone my lunchbox that had the Ninja Turtles on it. I had fallen into my mom's habit of calling these children I hadn't yet met my "friends" already, but as the condition of my cast worsened, I became deeply upset at the thought that surely I wouldn't be able to apply that label to anyone by the time this day was over.

When I realized that attempting to wipe the cast dry was actually destroying it, I wrapped the towel around my arm and pressed it hard against my chest while leaning forcefully against the counter, in an effort to soak up the water without agitating the surface of the cast. But the wet plaster began to collapse under my weight, and the force transferred down to my weak and cracked bones. Pain arced through my arm, and I half-successfully stifled a scream. I couldn't fix it myself. Defeated, I showed my mom.

It took thirty minutes to get most of the moisture out while working to preserve the rest of the cast. The combination of placing restrained pressure on an absorbent cloth while running a hair dryer over the length of the cast was enough to solve the hydration issue. To address the problem of the smell, my mom cut slivers off a bar of soap and slid them down into the cast. She then rubbed the remainder of the soap on the outside in an attempt to cocoon the rancid smell inside of a more pleasant one. There was no repair work that could be done, but she had at least controlled the damage.

By the time we arrived at the school, my classmates were already engaged in their second activity, and the teacher shoehorned me into one of the already-established groups. I'm sure that the teacher explained to me in great detail what the guidelines of the activity were, but I was so nervous and distracted that I must have misunderstood. Within about five minutes, I had violated the rules so badly that each member of the group complained to the teacher and asked why I had to be in *their* group. The teacher tried to make peace, but the damage was done; I sat at the table with my free hand in my pocket. I had brought a marker to school in hopes that I could collect some signatures or drawings on my cast next to my mother's, and as I rolled the marker between my fingertips, I suddenly felt very foolish for having even put it in my pocket that morning.

After the exercise was over, we watched as our teacher brought a large, rolled-up piece of paper out of the classroom's closet. While it is generally difficult to maintain the attention of so many children, the size of the object held our interest. We watched as she tacked the top and bottom left-hand corners of the paper to the wall as she talked to us. When the corners were secure, she unrolled the large cylinder of paper from left to right, and we saw what it was.

It was a map.

The teacher had us line up to leave the classroom for lunch. When we filed into the lunchroom, the faculty members from each Group guided us to our cluster of tables and corrected students who tried to sit at restricted, yet unoccupied seats. There were no other students in there; kindergarteners had the lunchroom to themselves at my elementary school, and this meant that I wouldn't have to sit by myself.

In a year's time, I would be all alone at a table about eight feet away, but despite the fact that I was surrounded by classmates, I think I felt lonelier right then than in all the initial weeks of first grade isolation combined.

One of the faculty members was making an announcement that no one seemed to be listening to while most of the kids were chatting energetically. I was eavesdropping on their conversations while self-consciously picking at the fraying ends of my cast when a kid sat across from me.

"I like your lunchbox," he said.

I could tell he was making fun of me, and I grew really angry; in my mind, that lunchbox was the last good thing about my day. I had used it every day at home since my mom had gotten it for me. She would make me sandwiches and put them in my lunchbox, and I would carry it to the white dining room table and eat them. It wasn't for practice; I was just excited to use it. Lunch that day in school was the first time I had used my lunchbox out of the house, and despite everything that had happened with my cast and the group earlier that day, I was still excited to use it officially.

I didn't look up from my arm to face my classmate because I felt a burning in my eyes from the tears that I was holding back. As I struggled to maintain my composure, I looked up to tell the kid to leave me alone. But before I could get the words out, I saw something that made me pause.

He had the exact same lunchbox.

I laughed. "I like your lunchbox too!"

"I think Michelangelo's the coolest," he said, while miming nun-chuck moves.

This was the first conversation I had ever had with another kid my own age that wasn't guided or chaperoned by my mother; while I had a lot of freedom in my neighborhood, there weren't any other kids that were my age, so when I played, I played alone. Even though this new dynamic made me slightly nervous, it was a good kind of nervous. I was speaking up to rebut his preference by saying that Raphael was my favorite, when he knocked his open carton of milk off the table and onto his lap.

"Aw. Crap!" he said, and immediately covered his mouth with both hands and reflexively shifted his eyes from side to side to see who might have heard it.

I tried very hard to stifle my laughter since I didn't know him at all, but the struggling look on my face must have struck him as funny because he started laughing first. Suddenly, I didn't feel so bad about my cast and thought that this person would hardly notice now anyway. As we laughed with one another, I thought to try my luck.

"Hey! Do you wanna sign my cast?"

As I worked the marker out of my pocket, he asked me how I broke my arm. I told him that I fell out of the tallest tree in my neighborhood, and he seemed impressed. I watched him laboriously draw his name on my cast – pausing before each letter to draw it in the air to make sure that it felt right. When he was done, I asked him what it said.

He told me it said "Josh."

Josh and I had lunch together every day, and whenever we could, we partnered up for projects. We became really close very quickly, to the point that if Josh was ever absent from school, I would feel a bit lost the entire day. We worked well together both within and outside of the curriculum of our grade. I helped him with his handwriting, and when I could, his spelling, and he took the blame when I wrote "Fart!" on the wall in permanent marker. I would come to know other kids, but I think I knew even then that Josh was my only real friend.

Moving a friendship outside of school when you are five years old is actually more difficult than most remember. The Friday we launched our balloons, the atmosphere was so energetic and excited that, when I had finished transcribing my letter, I joined Josh at his desk and asked him if he wanted to come to my house after school to play and maybe even stay the night. He said he did and that he'd bring some of his toys. I said that we could also go exploring in the woods around my house.

When I got home, I asked my mom if Josh could come to our house, and she said that would be fine. My enthusiasm was boundless until I realized that I had no way of contacting Josh to tell him. I spent the whole weekend worrying that our friendship would be dissolved by Monday.

When I saw him after the weekend, I was relieved to find that he had run into the same obstacle and thought that it was funny. Later that week, we both remembered to write down our phone numbers at home and then exchange them at school. My mom spoke with Josh's dad, and it was decided that she would pick up Josh and me from school that Friday. We alternated this basic structure nearly every weekend. If we managed to make plans far enough in advance, we would even secure permission slips from our parents so that we could just get off the bus with each other at either his or my house. The fact that we lived so close to one another made the arrangements much easier for our parents, who seemed to work constantly.

As time moved along, I found it more difficult to imagine doing things without Josh. That's not to say I actively tried to imagine such things, but as an only child, I had never had the disposition to picture myself with anyone else, except maybe my mother. As Josh and I grew closer, however, whenever I thought of a new place to go or a new activity to try, I always reflexively inserted Josh into the scenario. We had so many adventures when I lived in my old house that I find it difficult to remember them all. The actual nature of what we were doing never really seemed to have any impact on how fun the activity was for us. As long as we were together, we had a good time.

When my mom and I moved across the city during the summer after first grade, I was sure that our friendship had seen its last day. As we drove away from the house that I had lived in my whole life, I felt a sadness that I knew wasn't just about a house – I was saying goodbye to my friend forever.

But, to my surprise and delight, Josh and I stayed close.

Despite the fact that we spent the majority of our time apart and only saw one another on weekends, we remained remarkably similar as we grew. Our personalities coalesced, our senses of humor complimented each other's, and we would often find that we had started liking new things independently. I would sometimes call Josh, or he would call me, to share information about some new TV show or toy, only to find that it was old news for the other. We even sounded enough alike that when I stayed with Josh he would sometimes call my mom pretending to be me; his success rate was impressive. My mom would sometimes joke that the only way she could tell us apart sometimes was by our hair – he had straight, dirty-blonde hair like his sister, while I had curly, dark brown hair like my mother.

One would think that the thing most likely to drive two young friends apart would be what's out of their control. I'm quite sure that many friendships have stagnated when one party is forced to move away – the parents thinking that their children will just make new friends. While I feared at the time that this would be the case for us, I think the catalyst of our gradual disengagement was my insistence that we sneak out to my old house to look for Boxes.

That night, perhaps because we were old enough to reflect on it appropriately, seemed to cause a rift between us; not a striking and violent rift, but a gradual one – like two continents parting ways. The weekend after our excursion, I invited Josh over to my house, in keeping with our tradition of alternating houses, but he said that he wasn't really feeling up to it. If I'm honest, neither was I, and so I didn't protest. But maybe I should have.

We began seeing progressively less of one another over the next year or so. Our time together had gone from once a week, to once a month, to once every couple of months. Unlike when we were kids, we seemed to struggle to find things to do or talk about. But it was all gradual enough that perhaps we didn't notice it, even if we might have felt it.

For my twelfth birthday, my mom threw a party for me. I hadn't made that many friends since we'd moved, so it wasn't a surprise party since my mom didn't know who to invite. I told the handful of kids with whom I had become acquainted, but I was fine with a smaller party; I didn't want to invite a person just because I recognized him in the hallway.

About a week before the party, I called Josh to see if he wanted to come. He said that he didn't think he could make it. My mom had planned a lot of games and activities – there would be a piñata, "pin the tail on the donkey," and she even convinced a coworker to come perform a part of his amateur magic show. It occurred to me as we sat on the phone in silence that Josh might think he was too old for these activities, and I tried to reassure him that he didn't have to play any of the games or watch the magician, but he said that he just didn't feel up to a party. He said, "Maybe some other time," and we hung up.

After the phone call, I told my mom that I didn't want to have a party. I told her that I was too old for those games and that magicians were for kids. I told her that the whole thing was a dumb idea that she never should have had. The conversation with Josh had hurt me tremendously, and, senselessly, the only thing that I could think to do was to try to hurt her. It didn't work, and she just smiled and put her arm on my shoulder and said, "It'll be fine, sweetheart." And, inexplicably, I felt better.

The day before the party, Josh called me in better spirits to say that he would be there. It had been several months since I had seen him, and I was excited that we would get to spend time together and not have to worry about what to do or what to talk about, since there would be activities. I wasn't sure why he had changed his mind, but it didn't really matter to me. He was coming.

The party went pretty well. My biggest concern was that Josh and the other kids wouldn't get along, but they seemed to like each other well enough. Josh was quieter than I hoped he'd be. He hadn't brought me a gift, and he apologized for that, but I told him that it wasn't a big deal – I was just glad that he was able to make it. I tried to start several conversations with him, but they seemed to keep reaching dead ends. I didn't know what else to do; I had acclimated to the timid disposition that he had developed over the last couple years, but I had hoped that things might be different that day.

I asked him what was wrong; I told him that I didn't get why things had become so awkward between us – they were never like that before. We used to hang out almost every week-end and talk on the phone every couple of days. I suspected that it all really was because of the night we snuck back to my old house, and even though I couldn't know for certain, my voice trembled and quaked as I told him that Boxes was my cat and that it wasn't fair for him to hold that night against me for so long. But he didn't say anything. At a loss, I asked him what happened to us. He looked up from staring at his shoes and just said,

"You left."

I was about to ask Josh what he meant by that when my mom yelled in from the other room that it was time to open presents. I forced a smile and walked into the dining room as they sang "Happy Birthday." There were a couple of wrapped boxes and a pile of cards, most of which were from my extended family, since they lived out of state. Most of the gifts were silly and forgettable, but I remember that a kid named Brian gave me a Mighty Max toy shaped like a snake that I kept for years afterwards.

My mom was insistent that I open all the cards and thank each person who had given one, because several years before on

Christmas, I had torn through the wrapping paper and envelopes with such fervor that I had destroyed any possibility of
discerning who had sent which gift or what amount of money.
We separated the ones that had been sent by mail and the ones
that had been brought that day so that my friends wouldn't
have to sit through me opening cards from people that they
had never met. Most of the cards from my friends had a few
dollars in them.

One envelope didn't have my name written on it, but it was
in the pile so I opened it. The card had some birthday balloons
on its face and seemed to be a card that had been received by
someone else who was now recycling it for my birthday, because
it was a little dingy. I actually appreciated the idea that it was
a reused card since I'd always thought that cards were silly. I
angled it so that the money wouldn't fall to the floor when I
opened it, but the only thing inside was the message that had
come printed in the card.

"I Love You."

Whoever had given me this card hadn't written anything
in it, but they had circled the message in pencil a couple
times.

I chuckled a little and said, "Gee, thanks for the awesome
card, mom."

She looked at me inquisitively, and then turned her attention to the card. She told me it wasn't from her and seemed
amused as she took the card from my hand and showed my
friends, looking at their faces, trying to discern who had played
the joke. None of the kids stepped forward, so my mom said,

"Don't worry, sweetheart; at least you know now that *two* people love you."

She followed that with an extremely prolonged and excruciating kiss on my forehead that transformed the group's bewilderment into hysteria. They were all laughing now, so it could have been any of them, but one of the boys named Mike seemed to be laughing the hardest. To become a participant rather than the subject of the gag, I said to him that just because he had given me that card, he shouldn't think that I'd kiss him later. He gave me a slightly bewildered look, and we all laughed; as I looked at Josh, I saw that he was finally smiling.

"Well, I think that gift might be the winner, but you have a couple more to open."

My mom slid another present in front of me. I was still feeling the tremors of suppressed chuckles in my abdomen as I tore the colorful paper away. When I saw the gift, however, there was no more laughter in me to stifle. My smile dropped as I looked at what I'd been given.

It was a pair of walkie-talkies.

"Well, go on! Show everyone!" my mother encouraged.

I held them up, and everyone seemed to approve, but as I drew my attention to Josh, I could see that he had turned a sickly shade of white. We locked eyes for a moment, and then he turned and walked into the kitchen. As I watched him dial a number on the corded phone attached to the wall, my mom whispered in my ear that she knew that Josh and I didn't talk as much since one of the walkie-talkies had broken, so she thought I'd like it. I was filled with an intense appreciation for

my mom's thoughtfulness, but this feeling was easily overpowered by the emotions resurrected by the returning memories I'd
tried so hard to bury.

While everyone was eating cake, I asked Josh whom he had
called. He told me he wasn't feeling well so he called his dad to
come get him. I understood that he wanted to leave, but it was
so hard to get Josh to come to my house that I, perhaps selfishly, wished that he would stay, despite how he was feeling. I
told him that I wished we could hang out more. I extended one
of the walkie-talkies to him, but he put his hand up in refusal.

Dejected, I said, "Well thanks for coming, I guess. I hope
I'll see you before my next birthday."

"I'm sorry ... I'll try to call you back more often. I really
will," he said.

The conversation stalled as we waited by my door for his
dad. The rest of the kids watched my mother's coworker perform
magic. Rather than sounds of amazement, most of the vocaliza-
tions were critical but in good fun. Despite the haranguing, the
magician and my mother seemed happy; perhaps it was exactly
what they had expected.

I repeatedly opened my mouth as if words would just pour
out and catch the interest of my friend, but I would silently
shut it each time. I looked at his face. Josh seemed genuinely
remorseful that he hadn't made more of an effort, but I thought
I perceived some other brooding emotion behind his regret,
though I couldn't tell what it was. As I stared at him, perhaps a
little too intensely, his mood seemed suddenly bolstered by an
idea that had struck him.

He looked over to me and said that he knew what he'd get me for my birthday – it would take a while, but he thought that I would really like it. I dismissed it outright. I told him it wasn't a big deal and that I didn't need a gift. But he insisted. He seemed in better spirits and apologized for being such a drag at my party. He said he would call me soon, and when I said that he didn't have to treat me like a baby, he told me that if he didn't bother to call, then he wasn't worth being friends with anyway.

There was a knock at the door. Josh opened it and stepped out of my house and next to his father, and I could see Veronica sitting in the truck waiting impatiently. I thought about giving Josh a hug, but realized that might be embarrassing for the both of us, so I just gave him a low five. He apologized again as he walked off; he said that he was tired and that he hadn't been sleeping well, and I asked him why that was. He turned back toward me and waved goodbye as he answered my question.

"I think I've been sleepwalking."

That was the last time I saw my friend, and a couple of months later he was gone.

Since I began this attempt to learn more about my child-hood, the relationship between my mother and me has grown increasingly strained. Each time she would give me a piece of my past, I could feel myself becoming more complete – the structure of my autobiography finally falling into place with the connecting of milestones or the introduction of a never-known fact – but I don't think I realized how much of herself she was losing in this process. Still, I thought we could take it. But maybe I was letting my wishes about the strength of our bond distort my perception of how strong it actually was; it's often the case that one cannot know the breaking point of a thing until that thing fractures.

The last conversation that I had with my mother left me with what I'll now share with you. I'm not sure where this last discussion, and all of the ones that preceded it, will leave me and my mom; I imagine that we will spend the rest of our lives attempting to repair what had taken a lifetime to build. She had put so much energy into keeping me safe, both physically and psychologically, but I think that the walls meant to insulate me from harm were also protecting her emotional stability. As the truth came pouring out the last time we spoke, I could hear a trembling in her voice that I think was a reverberation of the collapse of her world. I don't imagine my mother and I will talk very much anymore, and while there are still some things I don't understand, I think I know enough now.

After Josh disappeared, his parents had done all that they could do to find him. From the very first day, the police had suggested that they contact all of the parents of the kids that knew Josh to see if he might be with them. They did this, of course, but no one had seen him or had any idea of where he might be. They placed notices in the newspaper and posted flyers all around the old neighborhood; they even solicited message boards and chat rooms in missing children networks.

The police had been unable to turn over any new information about Josh's whereabouts, despite the fact that they had received several anonymous phone calls from a woman urging them to compare this case with the stalking case that had been opened about six years before.

One day, however, they got a call. The person said that he had seen Josh. Josh's father sat down on the couch with his wife. Holding a pen to a pad of paper, he asked the caller where he had seen the boy. The caller said, "In Florida." The father pressed further, "Where? Where in Florida did you see him?" The caller yelled, "At Disneyworld!" laughed, and hung up.

His wife was clutching his free hand waiting for the information. She asked what the person had said, and Josh's father tore the piece of paper that read "Florida. Dis—" out of the pad and crumpled it up.

"Nothing. It was nothing."

These calls persisted for months. People from all over the country would call and offer fake tips or brutal mockery. There weren't many of these calls – maybe a dozen. But there were enough. They couldn't just change the number – Josh might call, or at least someone who had actually seen him – so they transferred the phone number to a friend who offered to act as a buffer from these kinds of callers. The friend said she would press anyone who asked about Josh, but otherwise she would just treat it as an ordinary wrong number. She was a good friend to them, and my mother struggled to remember her name, but I already knew it from the time that I had talked to her. Her name was Claire.

Josh's mother was not as strong as her husband was. If her grip on the world loosened when her son vanished, it broke when Veronica died. She had seen many people die at the hospital, but there is no amount of desensitization that can fortify a person against the death of her own child. She would visit Veronica twice a day, since she was recuperating at a different hospital: once before her shift, and once afterward.

On the day Veronica died, her mother was late leaving work, and by the time she arrived at her daughter's hospital, Veronica had already passed. This was too much for her, and over the next couple of weeks, she became increasingly more unstable. She stopped going to work, but unlike the leave of absence she had taken almost three years before when Josh had disappeared, this time she had nothing to focus her attention on except her own pain. She would sometimes wander outside yelling for both Josh and Veronica to come home, and there were several times her husband found her staggering around my old neighborhood in the middle of the night, half-clothed and frantically searching for her son and daughter.

Due to his wife's mental deterioration, Josh's dad could no longer travel for work, and so he began taking construction jobs that were less lucrative in an effort to be closer to home. When they began expanding my old neighborhood more, about three months after Veronica died, Josh's dad applied for literally every position that was vacant. He was hired.

Although he was qualified to lead the build sites, he took a job as a laborer. He would help build the frames and clean up the sites and do whatever else needed to be done. He even took odd jobs that would occasionally come up: mowing lawns, repairing fences – anything to keep from traveling. When they began clearing the woods in the area next to the tributary in order to transform the land into inhabitable property, Josh's dad was tasked with the responsibility of leveling the recently deforested lot; he accepted it eagerly, as this job guaranteed him at least several weeks of work close to home.

On the fourth day, he arrived at a spot that he could not level. Each time he would drive over it with the machine, the patch of land would remain lower than all the surrounding earth. Frustrated, he got off the tractor to survey the area. He was tempted to simply pack more dirt into the depression, but he knew that would only be an aesthetic and temporary solution. He had worked construction for years, and he knew that root systems from large trees that had been recently cut down would often decompose, leaving weaknesses in the soil below that would manifest as weaknesses in the foundations above.

Part of his motivation to do the job thoroughly was out of self-interest – with any luck he would be contracted to help with the building, or at least placing, of the future homes on this property, so he didn't want to sabotage himself. But this was only a small part of his reasoning. Ultimately, he was a builder; ignoring the problem was simply not a possibility. He weighed his options and elected to dig a little with a shovel in case the problem was shallow enough to fix without needing the backhoe that he would have to retrieve from another site.

I asked my mother where this site was, but it was almost a rhetorical question. I knew where it was. I had been to that spot before the soil was broken and before it had been filled in; I had fallen in that hole when I was ten years old.

I felt a tightening in my chest as my mother continued.

He stabbed his shovel into the dirt to test its consistency, and to his surprise and disappointment, the shovelhead disappeared almost entirely below the earth. The soil was weak, and while that would make it easier to move, he had not anticipated what might be such an extensive delay so soon into the job.

Pulling back on the wooden handle, he moved a small mound of dirt off to the side and began his project. Before too long, he had dug a small hole about three feet down. When he reset his position and drove the metal blade into the earth, a tremor traveled up the pole and into his arms. His shovel had collided with something hard. He smashed his shovel against it repeatedly in an attempt to gauge the thickness of the root and the density of the network, when suddenly his shovel plunged through the resistance.

Confused, he dug the hole wider. After about a half-hour of excavating, he found himself standing on a brown blanket that was stretched across and stapled to a large box about seven feet long and four feet wide.

Our minds work hard to avoid dissonance – if we hold a belief strongly enough, our minds will forcefully reject conflicting evidence so that we can maintain the integrity of our understanding of the world. Up until the very next moment, despite what all reason would have indicated – despite the fact that some small but suffocated part of him understood what was supporting his weight – this man believed – he *knew* – his son was still alive.

My mom received a call at six o'clock in the evening. She knew who it was, but she couldn't understand what he was saying. However, what she did comprehend made her leave immediately.

"Down here … now … son … please God!"

When she arrived, she found Josh's dad sitting perfectly still with his back to the hole. He was holding the shovel so tightly it seemed that it might snap, and he was staring straight ahead with eyes that had no life or light in them. My mother approached him slowly and tried several times to get his attention, but he wouldn't respond to any of her words. He only reacted when she tried, with delicate and hesitant hands, to take the shovel from him.

When she touched the shovel, his vice-like grip on the handle tightened, forcing all the blood out of his fingers to the point that they were as white as bone. He dragged his eyes slowly to hers and just said, "I don't understand." He repeated this as if he had forgotten all other words, and my mother could hear him still muttering it as she walked past both him and scraps of broken wood to look in the hole.

My mother told me that she wished that she had gouged her eyes out before she faced downward into that crater, and I told her that I knew what she was about to say and that she need not continue. I looked at her face; it was expressing a look of such intense despair that it caused my stomach to turn. It struck me that she had known of this for almost ten years and was hoping that she'd never have to tell me. I imagine that she made a firm decision all those years ago to never share this information, and as we sat there at the same weathered table that had forever been the meeting spot for our talks, I felt a twinge of guilt for forcing her to break the promise that she made to herself. Because she never intended to tell me, she never came up with the proper arrangement of words to describe what she saw. As I sit here now, I'm met with the same difficulty of articulation, but for different reasons.

Josh was dead. His face was sunken in and contorted in such a way that it was as if the misery and hopelessness of all the world had been transferred to it. The assaulting smell of decay rose from the crypt, and my mother had to cover her nose and mouth to keep from vomiting. His skin was cracked, almost crocodilian, and a stream of blood followed these lines and dried on his face while pooling and staining the wood around his head. My mother wanted to look away. She wanted to move her eyes, even if just a little bit, so that she could see something else, anything else. But she couldn't. Her eyes had locked with Josh's, which lay open and facing up out of the tomb, and although he couldn't return her gaze, it felt as if he were looking directly at her.

She said by the look of him he had not been long-dead, but she couldn't hazard a guess because she simply had no referent. Selfishly, and horribly, she wished that more time had passed before that day, so that time and nature could have brought the mercy of degradation to erase the pain and terror that was now etched into his face. She said that it felt as if he knew she'd be right there – that he had been waiting for her to enter his line of sight; his open mouth offering an all-too-late plea for help to ears that could do nothing for him. She forcefully covered her eyes to break the stare and attempted to confront the scene as a whole, but the rest of his body wasn't visible.

Someone else was covering it.

He was large and lay facedown on top of Josh. As my mother's mind stretched itself to take in what her eyes were attempting to tell her, she became aware of the significance of the way in which he laid.

He was *holding* Josh.

Their legs lay frozen by death, but entangled like vines in some lush, tropical forest. One arm rested under Josh's neck only to wrap around his body so that they might lay closer still, while the other arm lay limp with a bent elbow against the wood, his fingers entangled in Josh's hair. The man's back was covered in dirt, and as she looked back to the area near Josh's head – ashamedly avoiding his gaze – she could see that some of this scattered earth had mixed with the blood and formed mud that lay still wet in the damp casket.

As the sun passed through the trees, its light reflected off something pinned to Josh's shirt. My mother stooped to one knee and raised the collar of her shirt over her nose so that she might block out the smell while she attempted to train her vision on the object rather than Josh's face. When she saw what had caught the sunlight, her legs abandoned her, and she nearly fell into the tomb.

It was a picture …

It was a picture of me as a child.

Gasping and trembling, she staggered backwards and collided with Josh's father, who still sat facing away from the hole. She understood why he had called her now, but she could not bring herself to tell him what she had kept from everyone for all these years, not that the information could do any good now anyway. Josh's family never knew about the night I had woken up in the woods. They never knew about the Polaroids; they never knew about the note she had found on my pillow. They never knew the real reason we had moved out of our old home with such haste.

She had moved us into a new house to protect my life, and she had kept all of these things a secret so that life might be a normal one. She had talked to the police; she knew now that she should have talked to Josh's parents, but there was nothing to say anymore. As she sat there resting her back against Josh's father's, he spoke.

"I can't tell my wife. I can't tell her that our … that our little boy—" his speech staggered in fits as he pressed his wet face into his dirt-caked hands. "She couldn't bear it …"

After a moment, he stood up, still shuddering, and lumbered toward the grave. With a final sob, he stepped down into the coffin and positioned himself over the dead man's body. Josh's dad was a big man, but not as big as the man in the box was; however, he seemed unable to grasp this fact. He grabbed the back of the man's collar and pulled hard – it was as if he intended to throw the man out of the grave in a singular motion. But the collar ripped, and the body fell back down on top of his son. As this happened, what air remained in Josh's lungs was violently forced out through his mouth, and the father shrieked as he both watched and heard his son's last, empty breath.

"You mother fucker!"

He grabbed the man by the shoulders and heaved him back until he was off Josh completely. With one final, straining motion, he shoved the man until the body sat awkwardly but upright against the wall of the grave. Josh's father rested his hands on his knees and breathed heavily and painfully as he looked down at his only son. He grunted with anger and turned his attention to the man, and my mother could see the rage disappear from his eyes as something else replaced it. He staggered back a step. And then another.

"Oh God ... Oh God. No. No, please God. Please God no! No! No!"

In a struggling but powerful movement, he lifted and pushed the corpse of the man completely out of the ground, and as he did this, there was the distinct sound of glass first hitting and then rolling against wood. It was a bottle. He picked it up and absently handed it to my mother.

It was ether.

"Oh, Josh." He sobbed as he cradled his son. "My boy ... my baby boy. Why is there so much blood? What did he do to you?!"

As my mother looked at the man who now lay facing upwards, a chill came over her as she realized that she was facing, for the first time, the person who had haunted our lives for over a decade. Everything about our lives had changed since this person had entered it, and she had lost so much sleep thinking about this man. When she pictured him, whether in waking life or a dream, he was always evil and always terrifying; the cries of Josh's father seemed to confirm her worst fears. But as she stared at his face, she thought that this didn't look like who she imagined at all – this was just ... a man.

As she looked upon his frozen expression, it actually looked serene. The corners of his lips were turned up only slightly; she saw that he was smiling. This wasn't the expected smile of a maniac from a film or horror story; it wasn't the smile of a demon, or the smile of a fiend. This was the smile of contentment or satisfaction. It was a smile of bliss.

It was a smile of love.

When she looked down from his face, she saw a tremendous wound on his neck from where the skin had been ripped out; she realized that this wound must have been the source of the blood that stained Josh's face and the wood upon which his head rested. Initially, she was relieved by the realization that the blood had not been Josh's. Perhaps he had suffered less, and in a strange way, this small comfort amidst the madness set her slightly at ease. She looked to Josh's father who sat in the coffin, still holding his son to his chest, and wondered if she should tell him; she wondered if this tiny consolation was worth distracting him from his own thoughts, whatever they might be.

She drew her eyes away for a moment to think, and they lingered on the scraps of wood that lay scattered to one side of the hole – many of them still connected to a large, brown blanket. She recognized that these pieces of wood must have been the top of the box that Josh's father had torn away before calling her. Her drifting eyes and wandering thoughts both suddenly focused on what she saw in the debris, and she realized that she had been wrong to hope for any comfort now, in this place. Her mind raced to make excuses for this object's existence, but she was too tired to listen to anything but the truth anymore. She stared at the metal handle that was screwed into one of the boards of wood. She brought a hand up to her mouth and whispered, almost as if she was afraid to remind the world of what had happened.

"They were alive."

Josh must have bitten the man's neck in a desperate attempt to get free, and although the man had died, Josh wasn't strong enough to move him. When my mother realized this, she began to cry at the thought of how long he might have laid there and how he must have felt. She shuddered at the thought that he wouldn't have even been able to see in that dark place.

She crouched down beside the man and looked through his pockets for some kind of identification, but she only found a piece of paper. On it was a stick figure drawing of a man holding hands with a small boy, and next to the boy were initials.

She told me that the initials were mine. She asked me if I understood what it might mean, and I lied to her and said that I did not.

As Josh's father carried his son out of the grave, my mom slid the piece of paper into her pocket and stood up. He was muttering that his son's hair had been dyed, but he wasn't talking to my mother; it seemed almost as if he had forgotten that she was there. When she looked at Josh, she understood what his father was saying – Josh's hair was now dark brown, though it looked almost black as it clung to itself, cemented by blood.

Josh's dad delicately laid his boy on the soft dirt and began gently pressing his hands against his son's pants to feel his pockets. My mother noticed that Josh was oddly dressed; his clothes were all far too small for a boy his size. As the father applied pressure to his son's left pocket, there was a crinkle. Carefully, he retrieved a folded piece of paper from Josh's pocket and slowly unfolded it, not knowing what it might be. As he was returning the paper to its original shape, a small key fell from its folds and onto the dirt. He picked it up and looked at it as if he expected it to say something to him. After a moment, he pushed it into his front pocket before returning his attention to the paper.

He studied it but was vexed. With no immediately mean-ingful information to be gained from it, he handed the piece of paper to my mother. She nervously accepted it, but she didn't recognize it either.

When I asked her what it was, she told me that it was a map, and I felt my heart shatter. Josh was finishing the map – that must have been his idea for my birthday present. He had resumed the expedition on his own. That was our first great adventure, and he had decided to finish it, for me … for us. Tears began streaming out of my eyes as I learned this, and I found myself desperately hoping that he hadn't been taken while working on it. Despite everything that had happened, he had kept the map in his pocket for almost three years.

She heard Josh's father grunt angrily and looked to see him pushing the man's body back into the ground. As he walked back toward the machine that had found this spot for him, he put his hand on a canister of gasoline and paused with his back toward my mother.

"You should go."

"I'm so sorry … Is there anything I can do?"

"It's not your fault … It was me … I did this."

"You can't think like that. There was nothi—"

"I did this!" he roared.

There was silence for a long time. He seemed to be searching for the right words, or maybe he was just searching for a decision about whether he wanted to say them at all. Finally, he continued, his voice flat with almost no emotion at all.

"About a month ago, I was cleaning up the site on the new development, a block over, when a guy approached me. He asked if I wanted to make some extra money. Well, with my wife not working, I'd take just about any job, so I asked him about it. He said that some kids had dug a bunch of holes on his property, and he offered me $100 to fill them in. I told him that was no problem; just tell me where and when. He said that he wanted to take some pictures for the insurance company first, but if I came back after 8:00 P.M. the next day, that would be fine; he said I'd have no problem finding the holes.

"I thought this guy was a sucker since I knew clearing that lot was coming up for the crew I was on, so someone would've had to do it anyway; I actually felt bad for taking his money. It didn't even look like he'd have $100, but he put the bill in my hand, and I did the job the next night. I've been so exhausted that I didn't even think about it after it was done. I didn't think about it ..."

There was a long pause as he seemed to lose control of his voice.

"I didn't think about it until today, when I pulled that same guy off of my son."

He pointed at the grave, and his emotions finally broke free again as tears fell from his eyes and mucus from his nose.

"He paid me $100 so that I would bury him with my boy ..."

It was as if saying it aloud forced him to accept what had happened, and he collapsed onto the ground in tears. My mother could think of nothing to say, so she stood there in silence for what felt like a lifetime as she tried to comprehend what he had just told her. She knew that he wouldn't tell his wife about any of this. My mother knew that this would be the only time when he could reach out for any comfort at all. She knelt down and held him while he cried for his son.

Finally, she asked what he would do about Josh – where he would take him. But all he said was, "His final resting place won't be here with this monster." He rose and stepped delicately around his boy while he walked toward the grave with the canister of gasoline in his hand.

My mother left what used to be my old woods, but what was now just a mausoleum with no walls. As she looked back when she reached her car, she could see black smoke billowing and diffusing against the amber sky, and she hoped against all hope that Josh's parents would be okay.

When my mother had finished her story, we sat in silence for a long time. I wanted to feel anger or agony, but I felt nothing but a hollow emptiness inside. As we sat there, I realized that Josh's parents had called my mother when Josh went missing; she must have lied to them in the same way that she lied to me. Josh's parents must still believe to this day that their son really ran away.

I stood up to leave. There was only one question that I had for my mother – only one thing I wanted to know from her, but she couldn't answer it; I don't know why I expected that she could. I left my mom's house without saying much else. I told her that I loved her and that I would talk to her soon, but I don't know what "soon" means for us now. I got into my car and left.

As I drove, that stupid riddle about going into the woods came back into my mind, and that was enough to make me feel again; I remembered Josh and me talking about it in those woods nearly half my lifetime ago. I cried so hard that I had to pull my car over, and I again asked the question that my mother had been unable to answer. I asked it aloud even though no one was around to answer it but me.

"Why Josh?"

It was supposed to be me. It had always been me. So why wasn't it when it mattered the most? Why did I wake up in the winter woods when I was a child instead of being entombed in them? Why couldn't it have stopped then, with me? But I'll never know the answer to this question. I'll never know why he just left me there. There's no one I can ask now. Maybe he just couldn't do it. He tried, but in the end, he was just too weak to take me.

As I sat there in my car on the side of the road, I struggled to breathe between my exhausted sobs. I collapsed on the steering wheel and whimpered that I wished that he had been stronger.

I understood now. As the story became clearer with each detail revealed through the conversations with my mother, I had watched the pieces all fall into place, but I still couldn't understand why it had all stopped so long ago. Why it had all simply ended. Sitting in my car that night, I saw it all clearly for the first time. As an adult, I could see the connections that were lost on a child who tends to see the world in snapshots rather than as a sequence. The picture was complete, but I wished I had never seen it at all. I left the gas station and drove the rest of the way home, and thought – which is all that's left for me to do anymore.

I think about Josh. I loved him then, and I love him even still. I miss him more now that I know I'll never see him again, and I find myself wishing that I had hugged him the last time I saw him. I wish that he could have stayed at my birthday party longer that day – even if we didn't say another word to one another, we could have just sat there. That would have been nice.

I think about Josh's parents – how much they had lost and how quickly that loss had come. They were good people, kind people. The father had called my mother that terrible day so that she could keep me safe, but no one had called him to help him protect Josh. His parents don't know about my connection to any of this, but I could never look them in the eyes now. We still live in the same town, and I worry every day that I'll run into them somewhere. I find myself hoping that I don't see them, and I feel sick when I have that thought.

I think about Veronica. I had only really come to know her later in my life, but for those brief few weeks, I think I had really loved her.

I think about my mother. She had tried so hard to protect me; she had done everything she could possibly do to keep me safe. She was stronger than I will ever be.

I think about what our lives might be like now if I had just let my balloon go with Chris', or even a single second sooner or later than I did. Maybe someone else would have found it and everyone would be okay. Maybe I'd still have my friend and his parents would still have a son. Josh had been missing for almost three years – almost a fifth of his life. I try to pretend that I don't know what the man might have done with Josh for all that time, just like I try to pretend that maybe Josh wasn't in the passenger's seat the night Veronica was hit. I find myself pretending a lot now.

But mostly, I just think about Josh. Sometimes I wish that he never sat across from me that day in kindergarten; that I'd never known what it was like to have a real friend. Sometimes I like to dream that he's in a better place now, but that's only a dream, and I know that. The world is a cruel place made crueler still by man. There would be no justice for my friend, no final confrontation, no vengeance; it's been over for almost a decade now for everyone but me.

I miss you, Josh. I'm sorry that you chose me, but I'll always cherish my memories of you.

We were explorers.

We were adventurers.

We were friends.

... the end will take care of itself.

DEPUTY FIELD REPORT — _____ County Sheriff's Department

1. Person Arrested		
Address		Sex
5. Witness		
Address		Place of E
Witness Joshua		**Con**
Address		Place of E
10. Tool or Weapon Used	11. Method Used to Commit Crime (Chee) Forcible ☐ No Force ☐	
13. Kind of Property Missing		
		IDEN
15. Property Recovered		**O**
16. Vehicle Used Make	Tag Number	Year – Model

18. Details of Incident

_____ stated that her six ye
school project. Attached to it was a lette
requested the finder send a letter to
has received 48 photos but no lett
    Yesterday, he and his friend, Josh
a dollar bill marked, "For Stamps", in
realized he was in many of them. Mo
    Today in the mail, his mother recei
their home. From the clothing they had o
seized to be processed for prints.
known, however, _____

Reviewed and Sign _____   Unfounded ⬜

Copy to sheriff

	2. Offense				3. Complaint Number	
of Birth	Stalking				49 3	
	4. Address of Scene					4A. District
		6. Date — Time Occurred	7. Date — Time Reported		8. Date — Time Arrived	
	9. Victim (Business)					

al Record
ED TO.

Address		Phone

Victim (Person)

Address		Phone
Place of Emp.		Phone

ON BUFFALO
co

Reporting Incident/Contacted

Address		Ph
Place of Emp.		Phone

Color	17. Number Offenders	Sex	Race	Age

son, _____ had launched a balloon as a

one dollar bill marked, "For stamps". Letter

his school _____ along with pictures. He

co _____

snow cone stand in his front yard. He Fou...

ash. He looked at the photos he had and

he was the focus of or appeared in 33 of them.

hoto of him and Josh taken in the woods by

photo was taken yesterday. All photos wer...

r to be a case of stalking; No suspects;

rest □   Closed ...

Penpal

12183531R00152

Made in the USA
San Bernardino, CA
09 June 2014